# MOSTLY FRIENDLY SPOOKS

# MOSTLY FRIENDLY SPOOKS

SIX ORIGINAL GHOST SHORT STORIES

CORA FOERSTNER

WOOD SORREL PRESS

*For Liz, who believes in ghosts*

# INTRODUCTION

Let me start out by saying, "I had a blast writing these stories." I love them. They are fun, mostly not scary, and sometimes silly.

I think everyone has something or more than one something that they don't believe is true, but they wish it were true. For example, I don't believe in reincarnation, but I love the idea. Wouldn't it be wonderful if we got a life do-over? Or time travel. Wow wouldn't that be amazing?

Ghosts are another of my "I wish they were real."

Doesn't the idea of ghosts sound exciting or at the very least interesting? Not the horrible kind of ghosts that for some reason want to terrorize people.

Once while traveling though some southern

states, we stopped on one of the American Civil War battlegrounds.

"Hey, a bit of history," I said to myself. "Let's go see it."

The scenery was gorgeous, rolling green fields, tall swaying trees, and more.

The beauty couldn't mask the depression that came over me or the feeling of intense loss and sadness. I chalked those feelings up to knowing the brutal history.

We'd been there about ten minutes, when my young son grabbed my hand and said, "Mommy, I don't like it here. I wanna leave." I completely agreed. That was the moment I believed something painful, horrible, and wrong hung over the battlefield.

Ghosts of the past? That I would believe.

Of course, I know there's no way of proving ghosts are real.

My writer theory is that ghosts are somehow trapped in a time glitch . . . yeah, there's not a technical name for my theory. They are just trapped and have to hang out with us. Maybe they are warning us to listen to our better angels.

Funny story about someone I know. They shall remain nameless to protect them. She lived in a house haunted by the former owner, an older woman, who was just around sometimes and weird stuff happened.

Like when this person's mother came to live with her and claimed, "The old lady keeps using my perfume." That, my friend, is an exact quotation. Believe me, only a ghost would be inclined to "borrow" that particular perfume.

I once lived in an apartment where the light would flicker or sometimes even turn off. I'd leave a room, turn the lights off, and when I returned, the lights were back on. I used to joke I had a ghost.

Yeah, I know, faulty or old wiring. I'm a story-teller so a ghost sounded WAY more interesting.

The stories in this collection came about because of my interest in ghosts. As the title explains, these are mostly friendly-ish ghosts. I hope you have as much fun reading them as I did writing them.

The six stories included in this collection are:

*A Haunted House?* A grad student winds up at a haunted house for a job interview. She hopes for an offer of more money. What she receives outweighs her greatest expectation.

*Maxine's Uninvited Guest:* Maxine tries to buy her dream house, but the sellers make strange demands. She must meet their requirements, or they'll turn down her offer. Can she put up with their stipulations? Is her dream house worth it?

*A Decent Man:* Lucas wakes up and discovers something frighteningly unusual. He stands in a cemetery, his feet planted on his own gravestone, and no one can see him.

*Haunted Cabin:* Four friends rent a modern cabin for the weekend. They arrive and find a derelict building on the brink of collapse. False advertisement, spooky, abandoned? No, terrifying describes their experience.

*The Unintended Hero:* Ask yourself, what would you do if you woke up in a strange place? If you didn't know what happened? Find out how Robert Ramsey puts the puzzle together.

*Finding Redemption:* Reggie, rich, selfish, and unbending, discovers another reality. Cynthia longs to be happy and wishes for the happy times when they first marriage. When the tragic and unexpected happens, they both must find redemption before it's too late.

Grab your favorite drink, put your feet up, and have fun reading *Mostly Friendly Spooks.*

Enjoy,
Cora, Fall 2025

CORA FOERSTNER
A Haunted House?
A Spooky Short Story

1

# A HAUNTED HOUSE?

## 1: HARPER

The moment Harper Armstrong stepped out of her blue Prius, the smell of pastries and coffee made her smile. Her mouth watered as she glanced across the street at Some Crust Bakery. She looked both ways for traffic. She'd have to wait for two cars to pass.

The temperature was already pushing upward, and the sun felt a little too hot on her cheeks. She guessed they weren't going to have Southern California's famous June Gloom weather this year. A lot of people moved to the Los Angeles area and were shocked when they experienced the month of June as overcast and chilly.

She couldn't remember the last June Gloom. A couple or more years ago at least.

She spotted Eric sitting outside Some Crust Bakery in Claremont, California. His eyes were shielded from the sun by a pair of pink sunglasses. He'd probably offer them to her and pull another pair of purple or green ones from his pocket.

Two coffee cups and two white paper sacks sat on the aluminum table. She smiled. He'd ordered her coffee. If the bakery hadn't sold out her favorite pastry, she was certain that inside one of the white paper bags was a chocolate croissant.

She waved as she hurried across the street. Some Crust Bakery was a small shop with little more than standing room inside. People didn't seem to mind.

On the weekends there was often a crowd waiting, the line going out the door. They made the best pastries in the area.

Everyone ordered inside and waited while the local college students behind the counter hustled to fill orders. The two or three tables inside filled up quickly. Harper and Eric preferred to sit at the tables on the sidewalk out front.

"You're the early bird," she said as she slid into the aluminum chair beside Eric.

He grinned, flashing his perfectly white straight teeth. He pushed the paper cup of coffee and one of the paper bags in her direction. She opened the bag and inhaled the magical aroma of fluffy pastry and chocolate. Her chair faced the street, so her back was to the wall of windows. Inside were glass display cases filled with pastries and the aroma of more baking in the back.

Before she'd left her little apartment, she looked in the mirror and said aloud, "You will not look around for that man." Of course, she took a sip of black coffee and slyly glanced inside the window looking for the handsome stranger. He wasn't there.

Eric's brown eyes studied her as if she were an exotic creature.

"You're looking for him. You said you weren't going to do that."

"I'm not. I was stretching my neck."

"I doubt that. What's your news? Your message sounded cryptic."

Harper bit into her croissant. "Umm, these are always perfect."

"You are so easy to please. Answer my question. I'm dying of curiosity. And your attire . . . are you trying for casual business?"

Harper glanced down at her white blouse and her black dress pants. She smiled and shrugged.

"Yes. That's exactly what I'm going for. If we are going to critique each other, you need a haircut."

He ran his fingers through his thick wavy black hair. "I'm going for the scraggly look. Tell me your news."

"I have an interview. Well, according to Professor Jenkins, I have the job if I want it. A widower friend of his asked for a student to go through documents and papers related to an old house. There might be a book involved. It's an all-summer job."

She sipped the hot coffee and took another bite of chocolate heaven. She knew Eric would pelt her with a ton of questions. She was hungry.

Harper leaned forward and whispered. "The pay is extraordinary. I'll be able to pay for next year's classes. I won't have to work, so I can spend all my free time on my doctorate. The widower wants an older student, not some young thing. Professor Jenkins' words."

"You are hardly in your dotage. What are you twenty-eight?"

"Well, I'm not eighteen or twenty."

Eric chuckled. "Be prepared for a boring summer. If he's a friend of the professor, expect gray hair, a cane, and lots of nose hairs." He paused and considered it. "Never mind. I don't think any of that will bother you."

"I'm not interested in men. So, old is perfect."

"You need to get over that." He lifted the bear claw to his mouth and stopped. "Hunk alert coming your way."

She turned her head ever so slightly and strained her eyes sideways to see who Eric was interested in now. Hunk alert was right. A tall, dark-haired, athletic man walked toward the bakery.

The hunk wasn't for Eric. He was the man she was wildly attracted to, but she'd never spoken to him. She sighed.

"You say you aren't interested in men, but you can't take your eyes off him. I suspect this is your favorite place because you come here to get a glimpse of him. Talk to him."

There was no sense in denying Eric's comment. She did often come here hoping he would show up.

"No," she whispered.

"Well, you lost your chance to make a connection. He went inside."

Harper glanced around. Three feet from them, the mysterious stranger reached for the door. He held it open for a couple coming out.

He looked right at her and smiled. Her heart pounded like a mad drummer.

"Good morning," he said in a deep, smooth-as-chocolate-cream-pie voice.

Her mouth froze in some sort of adolescent freak-out as he slipped inside the shop.

"What is wrong with you?" Eric lightly slapped her arm.

"Nothing. I'm not interested."

"You lie like a silver-tongued snake."

She sighed. "When he comes out, look at his hand. He's married."

Harper couldn't resist turning her head and glancing inside the shop. His gaze met hers again. She quickly looked away.

"So, you have morals. I can't fault you for that," Eric said. "I can see the ring from here. He's definitely attracted to you." He leaned back and grinned. "Maybe he's attracted to me?"

"He's married," she said.

"I have questionable morals." He sighed. "You're right. Even my morals can't get past married. Sorry. Perhaps we should stop coming here?"

"Maybe. I am torturing myself a little. Plus, we should go somewhere for you."

"I'm fine. I don't freeze like a gazelle when a

handsome man says hello. I've been on three dates with a very attractive man, who doesn't mind when I talk nonstop about old bones and archeology."

"Who is he? Do I know him?"

"No, you don't know him. I won't say who he is until after six dates. A thing isn't a thing until at least six dates."

"I shall use my deductive skills and discover who he is." Harper glanced at her watch. "Gotta go. Don't want to be late."

"Hey, where's this job?"

"Ganesha Hills. Room and board for the summer."

He grinned. "I approve. If you want to entice a rich old guy with nose hairs, I can teach him to groom those hair. Wait, you have morals. I forgot."

She stood up. "I really gotta go."

He stood and kissed her cheek. "To make mister handsome jealous."

She resisted the urge to look toward the window.

She'd only taken a few steps when Eric called out. "If this old guy lives in the haunted house, don't take the job. That place freaks me out."

"The chances of that are minute." She chuckled and headed for her car.

She hadn't thought about the haunted house in years.

## 2. LIAM

Liam Johnson leaned against his car. There was a little shade from the building, but his suit jacket was too hot for the weather. He took the jacket off and tossed it on the front seat.

His cell rang. By the time he fished it out of his pocket, the ringing had stopped. The call went to voicemail.

He glanced down the street and saw her, the woman he'd never met. She was the main reason he frequented the bakery. Every time he saw her, he hoped to casually start a conversation. Somehow that never worked out.

The phone beeped. His sister's message was short. "Call me back as soon as you get this. It's important."

He hung up and glanced around. Now she sat outside the bakery with a man he had seen her with several times. He felt a moment's disappointment. If this man was her boyfriend, he probably didn't have a chance. He was buff, fit, and handsome.

He strolled toward the bakery. The aroma of

coffee filled the air. He loved Claremont. The streets and buildings were always clean and the common areas manicured. The main street looked like a small town, little shops, trendy places to eat, and a wholesome atmosphere.

The town was a nice surprise. The bakery was a gem. The coffee was okay. He didn't think anyone came for the coffee.

He came to see this beautiful woman and get a chance to talk to her. He'd been attracted to her the moment he saw her. Actually, the moment she bumped into him, he spilled coffee all over her T-shirt.

Her eyes were so blue they had hypnotized him for a moment. She apologized and scurried out the door before he could stop her. Since then, she seemed to disappear. He almost wondered if she was avoiding him, but he hoped that was wrong.

He'd caught her watching him. He wasn't certain but he hoped her glances were because of a mutual attraction.

When he reached the door to the bakery, she glanced up at him. He met her gaze. Oh, yeah, she was beautiful.

"Hi," Liam said.

She stared and didn't respond.

"Hi," her companion said.

He nodded and entered the bakery. Well, that was a bust. Either she was really shy, or she didn't want to talk to him. He glanced back. She was talking to the man.

His phone rang. He stepped in line, and answered his cell. By the time he reached the counter, he'd hung up. His server's badge said Sam.

Sam grabbed one of the white bags sitting on the counter.

"Here you go. Jelly donut, and coffee with milk coming up."

While the server got his coffee, Liam glanced back at the woman. Sam cleared his throat and put the coffee on the counter. He grinned and winked.

"That was fast," Liam said, feeling a little like Sam knew exactly what he'd been thinking.

"I saw you come in. You always order the same thing. And, you are always interested in her." He pointed with his chin.

Liam didn't bother to glance her way. "I didn't realize I was so transparent."

The server shrugged. "She's into you too. I've got a good sense for these things."

"Well, I think she has a boyfriend."

"And you are married." He pointed to Liam's wedding ring.

"I'm a widower. Two years. I've never taken the ring off."

"Take it off," Sam whispered. "She's not the kind who would date a married man. Eric's not her boyfriend. They're friends only."

"Thanks," Liam said.

He stepped away from the counter and moved toward the door. He should have asked her name. But Sam was talking to another customer.

Plus, his secret crush just stood up. Liam watched as Eric kissed her on the cheek and said something to her as she walked away. She waved and hurried across the street.

Kiss on the cheek. That could be friendship, or something else.

Liam stepped outside with his coffee. This was his chance to meet the friend and something might come of it.

"Eric, right?"

Eric took off his sunglasses, frowned, and squinted at him. A moment before Liam would have described his eyes as clear chocolate brown. Now his pupils looked dark. Clearly he was off to a bad start with her friend.

"I'm curious about why you think that's my name."

"Well, Sam, the guy who served me called you Eric."

He glanced into the bakery and stared at Sam.

Liam put his coffee on the table. "Look. I don't want to get Sam in trouble. Actually, I've been trying to meet your friend. I thought you two were a couple. Sam said you weren't. I thought maybe I could . . . talk to you?"

Eric's frown deepened. Liam sat down.

"I can see you are looking out for her. I admire that. I'll answer any questions you want to ask."

This wasn't as easy as he thought it was going to be. Plus, he was pretty sure he just got Sam in trouble for gossiping.

Eric stared at him for a few moments. "Okay. Why does a married man want to meet my friend?"

"Good question. I'm not married. My wife died two years ago."

Liam looked down at his hand, wondering if he should take a chance and let this guy into his private business.

Eric folded his arms. "Sounds like a scam. Grieving husband."

"Sure. Could be, but it's not. We married young.

Cancer took her too early. At first, I thought I was going to go crazy. After a year or so, that got better. I just never took the ring off. I wasn't ready to let anyone else into my life, so I kept wearing it."

"Sam tell you I was a sucker for sob stories?"

Liam shook his head and chuckled. "Nope. I was in line to get my coffee. It was a very short conversation."

Liam's cell vibrated. He glanced at the caller ID.

"You mind if I get his? It's my sister. She's interviewing someone for me."

Eric nodded.

"Hey, Sis."

"She's here. I really like her. She wants to tour the house, and she wants to meet you before she confirms. You should come meet her. I'll have lunch ready."

"Good idea. Hold on a second."

He placed his hand over the mic on his phone and glanced at Eric.

"This is kind of out there, but are you free for lunch?"

"Maybe. What did you have in mind?"

"I was supposed to interview someone this morning. I had my sister do the interview. The woman wants to meet me before she makes a final decision. My sister suggested lunch. I thought you could get to know my sister, see where I live . . . maybe you'd feel more comfortable about me."

Liam pulled out his card and wrote the new address on the back and handed Eric the card.

"Here's my address."

Eric glanced at the card and grinned. "Has anyone ever told you that you are a little too trusting?"

"Normally, I'm more cautious, but I'm taking a chance here."

"Because you want to meet my friend."

Liam nodded.

"Well, you've got balls. If anything happens, I know your name and your residence. So, is this your house or you rent?"

Liam sipped his coffee and looked at Eric. "You're very, very cautious and a bit suspicious."

"I am. Even in California a gay man learns to be careful. You gonna answer my question?"

"Sure, but my sister's waiting. Lunch?"

Eric nodded.

"Four for lunch."

He hung up and considered Eric. He'd never done anything like this before.

"I inherited the house from my great, great uncle.

He's the grandson of the woman who built the house. I'm fixing it up as part of a requirement in the will."

Eric glanced at the card again and squinted. "You rich? This is a fancy neighborhood."

"Wow. That's your question."

"Yes," Eric said. "So?"

"Why the question?"

"It's an upper-income neighborhood. I'm less interested in your money than I am in the house. I'm an architecture major. I know the house and the neighborhood."

Eric glanced at the window. Waved his hand and held up two fingers.

Liam was curious about Eric. Something kind of weird was going on. Usually he could read people accurately. At first, he thought Eric was an average guy, but it was weird he was so interested in the house.

Sam stepped outside carrying two iced drinks. He set them on the table.

"Strawberry lemonade. On the house," Sam said.

Eric winked at him and grinned. "Thanks." When Sam returned to the bakery, Eric sipped his lemonade and leaned forward.

"Your house is haunted. There's a curse on it."

Liam stood up. "You're sounding a little strange."

"Do I sound any stranger than you coming out here asking about my friend and saying you want to get to know me?"

Liam looked at Eric, who took a long drink and waited. The man had a point. This entire conversation was odd. Liam sat back down and took a drink of lemonade. It was good, tart and sweet. The strawberry tasted like real strawberries, not syrup.

"That sounds crazy."

"My hobby is studying haunted houses," Eric said.

"Haunted?"

"Yep, haunted. It was a dare. Go into the haunted house and see the ghosts."

"Did you see a ghost? In my house?" Liam decided to humor him.

"We saw something. My friend thinks there were two ghosts. Something or someone big and strong tossed three large stones at us. The noise boomed all over the block. One almost hit me. We ran for our lives. Actually, I screamed like a little girl. I don't believe in ghosts, but there's something scary about the house. Now, are you rich?"

Liam wondered if this banter was like arm

wrestling to see who's strongest, or in this case who's craziest.

"I'm not rich, but I'm not poor either. Middle of the road okay-ish. I inherited the house along with a trust to fix it up and follow my uncle's wishes."

"You're the administrator of the trust?"

Liam nodded.

"And this person you're hiring, what's their job?"

"Really? Isn't that my business?"

"Yes, but answer anyway. I guarantee you'll understand why later."

Liam took a long drink of lemonade. He hoped meeting this woman was worth all this. It was getting hotter and closer to lunch time.

"How do I know you're not some con man?"

"You're just going to have to trust me. I'll tell you everything at lunch."

Liam took a deep breath. This guy was annoying, but he'd put up with the questions to meet her.

"My great, great uncle built the house. According to the trust, there are lots of historical documents, house plans, etc. that need to be organized. My uncle was a writer. He said in his will that he wants all the history, oral and written, organized and catalogued. I'm hiring a grad student to gather all the documents, organize them, and if she's good enough, I'll hire her to write a book about the house. We are also turning the house and grounds into a writers' retreat and for writing seminars."

Eric stood and smiled. "What time is lunch?"

"Noon. Less than an hour. You can follow me and meet my sister. Since you're so interested in the house, she can give you a tour while I talk to the grad student."

"Excellent. How about I ride with you? I'm pretty sure I'll have a ride home."


## 3: HARPER

Ganesha Hills was a suburban neighborhood situated in the foothills of the San Gabriel Mountains. The houses overlooked the Pomona Valley. Realtors gushed that homes here had exceptional views. Harper couldn't fault them with their description.

She could see the whole breathtaking valley from here. Below, cars and trucks on the 10 Freeway whizzed past. Tract homes dotted the area beyond the freeway.

If a person knew where to look, and she did know, they could see Cal Poly University hugging the freeway. The administration building, shaped like a giant phallic symbol, jetted into the skyline taller than all the other buildings. She could spot the citrus groves at the university.

All the homes in Ganesha Hills were large and expensive. They were not cookie cutters. They had individual personalities and styles. There were plenty of 1950s tri-level homes that seemed more dated than many of the older homes.

Suddenly nervous about the interview, Harper circled the block twice before she parked her blue Prius. She stared across the street and smiled. She knew this house.

She double checked the address. The numbers on her paper were the same as the street numbers.

This was the haunted house of her youth. No, it wasn't built in the spooky old Queen Anne style. It wasn't falling apart with broken windows and a sagging roof. It was an exotic hybrid Mediterranean style. She doubted anyone thought of a haunted house or ghosts when they saw the place.

She'd grown up in the valley below. When she was young, her grandmother and everyone else said this house was cursed and haunted. Over the years, six people had died . . . of mysterious circumstances.

Harper wasn't a believer in curses or ghosts. The

house had been built almost a hundred years ago. People die. A hundred years had passed. It would be crazy if people didn't die.

It was built circa 1930. A wealthy widow commissioned it. She wanted a one-of-a-kind house, so the architect  designed it to represent styles from Spain, Italy, France, Northern Africa, and the Mediterranean Sea region.

The only reason Harper knew all that was because she had written a report on the house when she was in the architecture program at Cal Poly, Pomona. She wrote the paper with the hope of getting a tour.

That didn't happen. But maybe now was the time.

When she was fourteen, Harper and three of her friends rode their bikes up here. They'd cycled around the neighborhood until dark. They had dared each other to go inside and confront the ghosts of those long dead.

At that time, the place had been vacant for a few years. An empty, ill-kept house added to the allure of ghost stories and curses.

That night as they approached the grounds, she and her friends giggled from nerves. In her case, she had to laugh or her fear would have taken over.

Even though the moon was full, the night seemed dark, bathing everything in an ominous gray. The wind whistled through the overgrown bushes and palm trees. They hid their bikes in the overgrown hedges.

She'd never forget that full moon. It looked like a big shiny grayish circle with a ring around it. She didn't know what the ring meant, but she figured it wasn't good. The light coming from the moon turned everything gray.

Staring up at the untrimmed Mexican fan palm trees, she shivered. The moon silhouetted the slender trunk that stretched toward the sky. The old, browning fronds looked creepy. Harper's grandmother said the dried fronds looked like fans, which is why they were called fan palm trees.

Even at fourteen, Harper thought they looked like a nasty, dried fire hazard. Plus, she knew that rats lived in those dry fronds, which is why people cut them off.

That night, her young teenage self swallowed and tasted the acid in her throat. That was her first real experience with fear-inducing acid.

When Eric started to climb the fence, he looked down and said, "Come on. Let's do this." He glanced right at her. "You guys scared?"

She remembered he sounded excited. He also knew she couldn't resist a challenge. She ignored the burning bile in her throat and climbed up the wrought iron fence with sweaty, slippery hands.

In the distance, a coyote howled. She pressed her lips closed so she wouldn't scream.

Eric got his pant leg caught in one of the spikes at the top of the fence. He squealed like a piglet as his pants ripped. He tumbled into the yard and skinned his cheek.

Eric rushed in first. She and the others hung back until Roger shrugged.

"What the heck, I'm going in," Roger said.

He marched slowly up the steps like someone about to die. When he stepped through the door Eric had left open, Roger disappeared from view. Harper glanced at Susie, who shook her head.

She couldn't very well leave her friend alone. They waited in the tiled courtyard.

The cool night air felt good on her hot face. The scent of jasmine lingered in the air. Someone close by was making popcorn. She wished she was home eating popped corn.

Down the street a dog yelped. She sent up a little prayer that the coyote didn't get the dog.

Then boom . . . boom . . . boom.

Crash. Then another crash.

The sounds echoed around them.

Eric hollered something she couldn't understand.

More booms.

They sounded like something heavy being dropped from the third story.

Susie started to scream. Harper covered her friend's mouth.

"Shhhh."

Eric and Roger flew out of the house. Flying wasn't an exaggeration or hyperbole.

They literally jumped over the porch and stairs in one leap and sprinted toward them.

"Run, run!" Eric said, as he waved his hand toward the gate.

Harper was the first one over the fence and the first one to grab her bike. As she jumped on her bike, the neighbors' porch lights turned on.

They made the downhill ride in record time. They arrived at Eric's house hyperventilating and looking as if they'd seen a ghost.

They jumped off their bikes and threw themselves on the front lawn. Harper stared up at the sky. The ring around the moon looked red.

That was the last time she'd seen the haunted house.

She sighed and double-checked the address and the numbers painted on the curb. Even if the numbers were off, this was the place. It didn't look like the house she remembered. In the bright sunlight everything looked normal.

The wrought iron gate stood open. The central courtyard was clean, tidy, and the fountain that had been filled with dirt and weeds years ago, was now clean. Water flowed out of the statue of a woman holding a water jar on her shoulder.

Harper stepped out of her car, smoothed out her white shirt. Her dress pants were made of some kind of fabric that never seemed to wrinkle. She was trying to look as professional as possible.

The sun felt hot compared to her air-conditioned car. Jasmine scent filled the air. The Mediterranean tile in the courtyard looked new as did the red tiles on the roof. On the side of the house scaffolding as high as the second story hugged the walls. A man in white overalls was painting the outside of the house.

The arched windows and the faded detailed art echoed back to the Moorish influence. There was something odd about the first-floor window arrangement.

She'd seen similar spacing in old houses with secret rooms.

Three palm trees grew taller than the roof. There were no old fronds that needed trimming. The wide green fronds spread out over the front door, shading the entry.

Harper couldn't hold back a smile as she approached the front door. Oh yeah, she was going inside.

As she stepped onto the covered porch where the red tiles and palms shaded the entrance, she heard an old rock and roll song she recognized from her parents' music, but she couldn't remember the title or the lyrics.

She crossed her fingers for luck and took a deep breath before knocking.


## 4: LIAM


It was five minutes to noon when Liam pulled into the driveway of his newly inherited home. He watched Eric, who stared with an awed expression of wonder.

Eric followed Liam inside. Liam understood Eric's fascination with the house. He and June, his sister, had spent weeks going through each room and evaluating what work needed to be done. The place was an old marvel.

The front terrace had built-in Italian tile seating. June loved the kitchen with its butler pantry, statuary niches. The reception hall's high ceiling was decorated with cornices and original light fixtures.

The master bedroom had the original iron railing, a long multi-windowed wall that faced the back of the property. It was the largest bedroom Liam had ever seen. Walnut flooring throughout the upper floors.

Every time Liam entered the house, he felt as if he'd stepped back in history. The master bedroom had a privacy dressing room with a sink and second closet.

He wondered why a husband and wife would need a private place to dress. He guessed it was a more modest time.

He thought the place should be filled with people. The excessively large empty room sounded hollow and museum-like.

He watched Eric as they walked toward the kitchen. He touched the walls, opened doors, and made pronouncements.

"A grand salon," he said. "Walnut pocket doors. The fireplace is Italian limestone."

He said "spectacular view" so many times that Liam rushed over and peered out the windows.

The views were spectacular. He'd been so busy trying to clean things up that he'd missed the beauty.

At the rate they moved toward the kitchen, he guessed his sister would be annoyed because whatever food she'd planned was probably cold.

"Come, Eric, we'll tour the house after lunch."

Eric rushed across the room, his face aglow with enthusiasm. "Excellent. This place is fabulous. It's going to cost a fortune to keep it up."

Liam had already figured that out. He hoped the trust would cover all present and future expenses.

They stepped into the enormous kitchen, which had been modernized and looked like something out of *Architect's Digest* with a stainless steel theme.

June stood at the sink drying her hands.

"Oh, there you are," she said.

His sister had been exhausted, but today she looked perky and cheery. She was two years older than he was. Her cheeks were rosy and her blond hair was in a ponytail. She wore jeans and a work T-shirt.

"Eric, this is June, my sister. Eric's an architectural student and enthusiastic about the house."

"Wonderful," she reached out and offered Eric her hand. "That makes two architectural students."

Liam glanced around looking for the woman he was going to interview.

"Oh, you're looking for Harper. She is in the library. She's found something interesting." June tossed the towel on the counter.

"A hidden room," Eric said.

June smiled. "Yes. How did you know?"

"The windows are oddly spaced."

"That's exactly what she said."

Liam headed for the kitchen door. He was anxious to see this hidden room.

"Come, June, this is going to be interesting," Eric said.

"I've already seen it. Another room to clean."

"This will be better than a room to clean."

Liam wondered at Eric's words. What could be more interesting than a hidden room? He quickened his pace, and heard Eric and June's footsteps behind him.

He rushed into the library, where he found one of the bookcases moved forward. Behind it was another room. Not large. It seemed like a mini library with old dusty shelves filled with books.

Two walls were covered in old paintings of various sizes. Liam guessed they would have been considered risqué back in the day. Naked women, men. A series of smaller paintings depicted a naked man and woman in very intimate poses.

Liam stopped and stared and tried to imagine the prim and proper woman he'd seen in pictures owning these paintings.

"They are quite shocking. Are they not?" June said. "For a great, great, great aunt."

"Even great, great, great aunts were young once," Eric said. "I believe a couple of these may be famous. Harper would know better than I would."

Liam turned toward his sister. "Where is this Harper person?"

Eric pointed to the far wall, where Harper had taped a note that pointed downward with a one-word message: STAIRS.

Liam rushed to the door and looked down. Electric lights placed every few feet lined the very, very long staircase and tunnel. Eric and June stood behind him.

"How big is this property?" Eric asked

"Two and a half acres," Liam said as he started down the stairs.

Behind him, Eric spoke to his sister. "Are you up for a long walk?"

"Do you think it's long?"

"I do, but I promise a surprise at the end," Eric said.

June laughed and took Eric's hand when he offered it to her. Eric was eccentric, and he'd somehow charmed Liam's sister in a few minutes. His odd statements reminded Liam of the Mad Hatter. He heard Eric whispering to his sister. She giggled.

Liam ignored them and hurried forward. He stepped into the bright sunlight. The woman he constantly thought about stood in front of him, shielding her eyes from the sun. She looked out over the wild vegetation and trees in this part of the land.

"Harper," June called.

"June, you made it. I think I've discovered the source of the ghosts and strange noises you've been hearing. You have squatters on your land. They might know how to get into the tunnel leading to the house."

Harper turned to face them. Her eyes widened.

"Oh, it's you." Her gaze moved past Liam. "Eric? What are you doing here? June, you know Eric?"

"Harper, I'd like to introduce you to Liam," Eric said. "Liam, Harper."

June stepped forward. "Is this your mystery woman?"

"Yes." He whispered and glanced at Eric. "You knew. You could have warned me."

"What would be the fun of that?"

June laughed.

## 5: HARPER

Six dates later, Harper sat across from Liam. They ate by candlelight, sitting on his large patio. Liam had made tacos because he'd discovered it was Harper's favorite meal, second only to a chocolate dessert.

She sipped from her glass of red wine and watched the man across from her. Every taco shell he bit into cracked and spilled lettuce, cheese, guacamole, and tomatoes onto his plate.

She smiled and held back the laughter that bubbled in the back of her throat.

"I should eat tacos with a fork," he said.

"I agree. Or cook with soft tortillas."

"The premade sounded less complicated."

His smile lit up his face. In the two months they'd known each other, she'd discovered how gentle and kind he was. Her attraction to him hadn't dimmed. Just looking at him made her feel warm all over.

He put his fork on his plate and took a very long swallow of wine which caused his lips to pucker.

"What are you doing?" she asked.

He held up his glass. "Getting some liquid courage. It's only been a couple months. I wanted to say that I'd like to stick with this dating trial we've been having and see if there's something more and deeper for us. What do you think?"

She let her smile widen. "Did you really have to ask that? Aren't my intentions obvious?"

"Yes, I did have to ask. Eric says a thing isn't a thing until we've had six dates."

She chuckled, "You're taking dating advice from Eric? Answer my questions."

"You said you wanted to go slow, so I'm asking if we can go a little bit faster. Is it too fast if I say I'm falling for you?"

She leaned across the table and kissed his warm, soft lips.

When they finally pulled apart, she said, "I'm falling for you, too."

She glanced up to the second floor where the lights had been off a moment ago. The lights were on. An older woman stood at the window, wearing a party dress that reminded Harper of the 1930s. When Liam turned and gazed up to see what Harper was looking at, the woman blew them a kiss and waved. Then she vanished.

"We might have to figure out how to get rid of the ghosts," Liam said.

"Or we can learn to live with them. Eric would be disappointed if they left."

"Then we'll have to set privacy guidelines."

Harper raised her glass. "I'll toast to that."

Their glasses touched and clinked just loud enough for the ghost dog at Liam's feet to raise his head and look around.

# CORA FOERSTNER

### Author of the Dragon Speakers Duology

# Maxine's Uninvited Guest

A Spooky Short Story

# MAXINE'S UNINVITED GUEST

## 1

Maxine Pari sat in Jill Roscoe's real estate office waiting for Jill to finish copying her paperwork. Through the window that separated the small office from the larger reception area, she watched Jill at the copy machine. The machine spat out paper at a remarkable speed. Jill watched the process as if mesmerized.

A little ball of anxiety flittered in Maxine's stomach. She'd fallen in love with a small house less than a half mile from the ocean. Standing on the front porch for the first time, she smelled the salty ocean air.

The moment she stepped into the house, she knew. This was it. She really, really wanted the house.

To keep her mind from obsessing about what might be wrong with the contract, Maxine surveyed Jill's office. The stuffy room smelled like a car with new air freshener that made Maxine's throat tickle. She quickly opened the office door to let in the cooler air from the reception area.

The office decor might have been ripped from an old 1940's noir private-eye movie, where the intrepid hero was on the verge of getting evicted. Jill must have chosen the decor purposefully because she didn't appear to be on the verge of eviction.

Nothing about the office reflected a successful business, which seemed weird since three separate people had recommended Jill as the best realtor. The carpet was old but clean, a row of metal file cabinets lined one wall. Jill said she didn't trust digital files. She also didn't trust voice messages, but text messages were fine.

The woman was a ball of eccentricities, but she'd worked hard to help Maxine find a house, going out of her way until they found the perfect home. She'd won Maxine's appreciation.

Now the big question was—were the owners stonewalling or raising the price or something else so strange that Jill was making her a copy of the contract the other realtor sent?

Maxine dabbed her forehead with a tissue from the desk. Even with the door open and some of the cool air from the reception area sneaking in, the rooms were too hot.

The copy machine stopped. Jill, with a frown that would have frightened small children, marched toward the office. Her body language caused Maxine to stand.

Jill, a short woman with short black hair that looked glued in place, made eye contact with Maxine. Her bright red lipstick seemed out of place as her frown deepened.

On her first visit, Maxine almost ran out the door, but Jill was one of those strange people who made other people feel as if everything would work out because she would make it so. Maxine stayed and discovered that Jill had three excellent qualities.

She had listened to what Maxine wanted, she found properties that were almost exactly what her client wanted. When they went to view the house,

Maxine noticed every single little repair that needed to be made. Then she somehow got the sellers to agree to fix everything.

Maxine fell in love with the little house. It wasn't too big or too small. Goldilocks would have been right at home.

The bid was accepted within an hour, which caused Maxine to wonder what was wrong with the house. From the look on Jill's face, she was about to find out.

Jill's message today simply said, "Got the contract. You need to come over ASAP. There are a few oddities."

Maxine tapped her foot like someone with restless leg syndrome. Jill's usual chipper personality had morphed into a morose dejection. There was a good possibility that Maxine wasn't going to like the contract.

Jill hurried into the office. She motioned Maxine to sit and slipped a handful of pages her way.

Maxine scanned the first page, which looked like standard contract legal jargon. Across from her, Jill grabbed the eyeglasses that dangled on the multicolored beaded necklace round her neck and slipped them onto her face. For a moment, her eyes looked huge. The magnifying effect vanished as quickly as it came.

With a dramatic sigh, she sat behind her generic circa 1945 desk. The army greenish metal desks reminded Maxine of an old desk her father used to keep in the garage. The odd thing was this desk looked brand new.

"You can read it if you want, but it might be quicker if I just give you the bad news. I have a feeling this might be a deal breaker."

Maxine's heart did a thump, thump of disappointment. Her A-fib could have been acting up, but she didn't think so. She swallowed and ignored the knot in her stomach. She really, really wanted to find a way to make this sale work.

"Are you saying there's something wrong with the structure of the house?"

"No. Well, not exactly. There are odd stipulations."

"Stipulations?" Maxine had never heard of stipulation in buying a house. "Can sellers make stipulations?"

"Yes, they can, but we can negotiate."

"Okay. Give me the bad news."

"Well, first there's Mr. Tibbs. He comes with the

house. He's a calico cat who has been with the house since."

Jill glanced at the paper in front of her. When she looked up, she was pressing her Santa Claus red lips together, looking very much like someone who was trying not to laugh.

"Umm, well . . . since 1978 when the house was built. Also, his great, great, great grandson, Sprinkles, comes with the house."

Several unsavory thoughts rushed through Maxine's mind.

She chose the least offensive and asked, "Are these cats stuffed like a taxidermist might do?"

"Well, um . . . no, they are not stuffed."

"Hold on. Cats don't live . . . what forty-plus years? Is this a joke?"

Jill rubbed her hand on her forehead as if a headache were brewing or percolating . . . whatever headaches did when a person wanted to run screaming from the room.

"Yes, it probably is, but the owners are serious. They believe Mr. Tibbs is a ghost cat. His grandson Sprinkles is still alive, but very old. They want Sprinkles to live his days out in the house where he was born."

Jill closed her eyes and sighed.

Maxine didn't know her well, but she knew her well enough to know that the worst news was yet to come.

"Let's skip to the chase. There's something worse that you don't want to tell me. Just say it," she said to Jill.

Jill placed her elbows on the desk, took off her glasses, and rubbed her hands over her face. Maxine had seen her father make those same movements just before his exasperation led him to raise his voice.

Jill didn't raise her voice. She whispered. "The house is haunted."

Maxine chuckled. The owners were pranksters or crazy. It would probably be better not to call them crazy.

Jill leaned back in her chair and looked at Maxine with a growing smile.

"So, the owners are eccentric?" Maxine asked.

"You could say that . . . there's more."

"I don't believe in ghosts. Sprinkles? He can stay. What else?"

"There is a list of foods to feed Sprinkles . . . and do you remember the smallish bedroom next to the kitchen."

Maxine nodded. It looked like something right out of a 1940s melodrama.

She realized that no one was going to come to the house and make sure she was feeding Sprinkles the exact food the owners fed him, nor was their ghost cat going to run to them complaining.

This suddenly turned into something quite entertaining. She wondered if this was why the house hadn't sold. She should have bid lower.

"Yes. Is that the ghost's room?"

Jill burst out laughing. "Yes. Yes, it is."

Maxine joined her. In a few seconds, both women's laughter turned to deep belly laughs. Finally, when they were both gasping for air, the laughter slowly died down.

Bill, the other agent who worked in the agency, stepped into the reception area and glanced over at them. He was an older man who had a rather pleasant smile. Maxine got the impression he knew about the agreement. He grinned knowingly, waved, and returned to his office.

"Jill, what's the stipulation with the ghost's room?"

"They want you to keep the room just as it is. You cannot use it yourself. Um, the old lady who built the house, prefers that room. She's the ghost.

According to page two, she's extremely picky and will not allow anyone in the room, except to clean."

She was buying a house from people who weren't completely sane. Later they would make a lovely story to entertain her friends. Her shoulders relaxed and she leaned back in her chair. These were simply silly requests.

"Who enforces these stipulations?" Maxine asked.

Jill shrugged and frowned. "Every three months for two years, the wife will stop by to make sure the grandmother ghost is happy and that Sprinkles has the proper food."

"No, not going to happen . . . can they do that?"

"No, but I suspect if you don't agree, they'll back out of the sale. I can, however, tell them you'll take care of Sprinkles until his death—"

"And tell them I don't mind the ghosts. Cat ghost and old lady ghost can stay. And, why would they want me to leave the room the way it is?"

Jill held her index finger up and grabbed the phone. After she dialed, she covered the receiver with her hand and whispered.

"I'm calling their realtor. He's a friend of mine."

Her index finger went up again. "Nick, it's Jill from Franklin's."

Maxine heard a jovial male voice and laughter. Jill grinned at her.

While Jill questioned Nick, Maxine picked up the contract and glanced through it. After a few seconds, Jill tapped her hand on the desk. The metal sounded like a distant drum.

"He wants me to put him on speaker phone. Is that all right?"

Maxine nodded.

"Go ahead."

"Hi. This is Nick."

Her mother had that habit on the phone, "Hi Max, this is your mother." She shrugged the similarity away.

"Hi," Maxine said.

"As you can see, the contract is a little crazy. They seriously believe their grandmother is a ghost and living in the house, in that small room. They insist you can't use it for anything else. I think I could get them to agree to one three month visit. You could leave the room alone and after that redecorate."

"Couldn't we just say no?"

"You could try, but others have balked, and they took the property off the market. They said that grandma gets very annoyed if her room is changed. Sprinkles is old, quiet, and just lies around all day as cats do. You could hire a lawyer to haggle with them, but I wouldn't recommend that. Three other people tried, and the Andersons backed out of those deals."

"Why exactly is he called Sprinkles?"

There was a long pause that confirmed her suspicions.

"From what I understand, he liked to play in the sprinklers when he was a kitten. Most cats don't like water so they thought his behavior was cute."

"Do you believe that?"

Jill grinned and winked at her.

"No way. It's probably what you are imagining, but I can't prove that."

Maxine thought she'd throw in another question for kicks. "Have you seen this ghost?"

Another long, very long pause, which had Jill sitting up straighter.

"Nick, are you still there?"

More silence.

"Yeah, I was drinking some water. I have a sore throat."

"Maxine asked about the ghost?" Jill winked at Maxine.

"Damnit. Yes, or no, or whatever. There was something in the room, but the owners are so creepy that it could have been my imagination. Just like a shape out of the corner of my eye, but it vanished."

Jill put her elbows on the desk, took off her glasses and rubbed her face.

"You're joking, right?" Maxine asked.

"Well, . . ."

"Nick, Stop! You are never going to sell that house if people think you've seen a ghost." Jill's eyes were wide as she shook her head.

"I can't say for sure."

"Then don't say anything."

Maxine leaned toward the phone.

"Nick, find out if they'll agree to one three month visit. I'll take care of the living cat and ignore the ghosts. Then that's it. I will not spend a year catering to them."

"Excellent," Nick said. "I'll call them now. I hope with all my heart this works."

And that final decision was how Maxine Pari bought the cute cottage half a mile from the beach. She believed she could put up with anything for three months.

2

Forty-five days after signing the contract for Maxine's new house, she spent one long day moving. The lovely pale green house with white trim located in the middle of Elm Street was hers.

The oak floors were clean and shiny. The kitchen's marble tops and large windows were also clean. She inspected the house, and the only thing unusual was the third bedroom, which still looked like a 1940s parlor. She reminded herself she only had three months of that nonsense, and she'd turn the room into a guest room or maybe even a home office.

Her brother, her best friend, and her sister helped her direct the movers to place boxes and furniture in the correct rooms.

Her sister, Sally, bossed the movers around so much that Maxine finally sent her out for a food and drink run. Her brother, Philip, kissed her on the cheek.

"Thank you, she was driving everyone crazy."

Finally everyone left. She sighed contentedly, and walked through the house soaking up all the atmosphere. The long narrow kitchen with its big windows looked out to a fair-sized backyard of grass. It wasn't particularly nice or well-tended grass, but that didn't matter. She planned to plant flowers, put in a small vegetable garden and more.

The master bedroom was large with a sliding glass door that led to the backyard, the other rooms were simply bedrooms. Both bathrooms would have to be remodeled someday, but that was for later.

She took a shower and put on the pajamas her sister had laid out for her. Every bone in her body felt achy and tired. She went to the kitchen for a bottle of water. On the way to her bedroom, she noticed a box of books had been opened. She hadn't opened it, probably Sally was looking for something.

When she went to close the box, she noticed that two books lay on the floor and her daily planner lay open on one of the closed boxes.

Sally wouldn't have done that. Adrenaline shot through her body, and an uncharacteristic fear made her wonder if someone had sneaked in while she walked her brother and sister to their cars.

She checked the front door, then the sliding door to the backyard, the sliding door in the kitchen, plus the regular kitchen door, and the sliding door in her bedroom.

She realized three sliding doors seemed excessive.

They were all locked. Then she checked the

windows. Everything was closed, locked, and nothing else was out of order.

Philip loved practical jokes. He'd even jokingly asked if she wanted him to stay the night to keep the ghosts at bay. She grabbed her phone and texted him.

Not Funny!

A few seconds later, he responded.

????

Opened boxes . . . really?

Not Me. Maybe Sally…

She knew he wouldn't admit to joking around. Of course, he couldn't last long without confessing. She would bide her time and think of a way of getting back at him.

The movers had set up her bed in the master bedroom. That night the full moon created just enough light through the curtainless window to chase the unfamiliar shadows away. She fell asleep from pure, delightful exhaustion.

She had barely dozed off when something

jumped onto her bed. She sat up with energy she hadn't had a second ago.

Right beside her sat a rather large black cat with what looked like a mustache. It stared at her. She had expected this.

"Oh, you must be Sprinkles," she said and petted him.

He didn't pull away, but he also didn't purr.

His fur was rather cold. He must have been outside. Tomorrow she would have to find the cat door. She wasn't sure how she felt about the cat coming and going.

She lay back down and closed her eyes and settled back into sleep.

She'd looked for the cat earlier but couldn't find him. The movers said he was probably hiding. She took their word for it and forgot about him.

Later she found his bowl, five cans of cat food, and a water fountain. She opened the cat food, and placed it in the bowl and added water to the fountain. She still hadn't seen the cat.

He must have been freaked out and hiding with so many people in the house. Now, he curled up at the foot of her bed.

That night she dreamed. In the dream, Sprinkles slept at the foot of her bed. Another cat, who looked like a whisper of smoke or a silhouette, joined him. The new cat curled up next to Sprinkles.

The dream seemed to fade away, but another dream replaced it. Her door opened and an elegant woman about fifty entered the room. She sat next to Maxine. In the dream, the bed even sagged when she sat.

"Wake up, dear." A very cold hand touched her shoulder.

"No," Maxine whispered.

When she was overly tired, she always had strange dreams. The key was to ignore them, or she'd find herself up all night.

"Wake up."

"Go away."

"Well, you are quite rude. What exactly do you think you are doing in my house?"

"Go away."

Maxine woke up shivering from the cold. She reached for the lamp that usually sat beside her bed. Empty air greeted her. She sat up, saw the moonlight, and the sliding glass door open.

She remembered where she was and was instantly awake. That door had been closed and locked when she went to bed. She locked it herself.

She got up.

Her heart pounded. The moonlight gave her just enough light to see outlines. She grabbed the bat Philip had placed beside her bed.

"In case the ghost appears. Muahahaha, " he'd said.

For once, his silliness came in handy. Bat in hand, she quickly closed the sliding glass door, locked it. Then she walked through the house making sure everything was locked. She checked every closet, each bathroom, and finally crawled into bed wide awake.

Sleep finally came just as the sun was painting the night sky.

Her cell's ringing and someone's pounding on the front door brought her fully awake. She fumbled under her pillow and found her phone

"Hello."

"Max," Sally said. "I've been pounding on your door for five minutes. Where are you? Why do you sound funny?"

"I was asleep. Hold on."

She hurried down the hall to the living room, where she stopped and stared. Half her boxes were opened, the things were scattered all over the room as if someone had been throwing things willy-nilly.

On the wall, someone had used a black marker to write:

Don't ever tell me to go away again!

Sally knocked on the front door. "Max, let me in."

After gaping at the wall for several seconds, Maxine stepped over a broken vase, a sofa pillow and made her way to the front door.

When she opened the door, Maxine stared at Sally whose hand was still raised. She juggled a cardboard cup holder with two cups of coffee in her other hand. A white paper bag from Bear Claws Are Us sat on the black mailbox that was attached to the porch wall. Sally stared at Maxine and glanced past her.

"What exactly is going on?" Sally grabbed the paper bag and handed it to Maxine.

She practically shoved Maxine out of the way as she rushed into the house. She glanced at the items scattered around the room and glanced back at Maxine.

"I don't know. I heard nothing."

Sally touched her round belly. She was six months pregnant and a few weeks ago started touching her belly whenever she seemed upset or annoyed. Right now she was probably both.

She had also stopped styling her hair and now

wore her blond curly hair in a ponytail that hung down past her shoulders.

She pointed to the message on the wall.

"Max, are you having some sort of psychic breakdown from the stress of buying this house?"

Maxine sighed, grabbed the coffee from Sally, and shook her head.

"Come on. Let's see if the kitchen is safe."

She watched Sally gingerly step over a vase. She kicked two pillows out of her way, and picked up a framed picture with broken glass. It was her favorite picture of their mother and father sitting on the beach in Florida where they'd moved when they retired. The most stereotypical thing they could have done. They returned to Southern California a year later.

The kitchen was exactly as she had left it. While they sat at the table eating donuts and sipping coffee, Maxine explained what had happened during the night.

When she finished, Sally frowned at her.

"You can't seriously believe in ghosts."

"No, Sally, I do not. Truthfully, I don't know what this is. I had weird dreams, maybe slept a few hours, and woke up to your knocking and the mess in the living room. Someone did this, but who and why?"

Sally took a huge bite of her bear claw and looked out the sliding glass window into the side yard.

Maxine wondered if she should say something about eating two giant bear claws. Sally always had a slender figure, but even someone with a fast metabolism could overdo things in the bear claws snack department. After about two seconds, she decided life would be better if she ignored her sister's eating habits.

"It's the crazy people you bought the house from."

Maxine took another sip of coffee. Maybe pregnancy had shifted Sally's hormones.

"Don't look at me like that," Sally said. "Consider the possibility. Isn't that more rational than ghosts and haunted houses. Today, we'll change the locks."

"By that you mean, we'll call a locksmith to change the locks."

Sally shrugged. Neither of them had any kind of DIY skills. She did have a point.

"Sally, why? Why would the previous owners do this?"

"Because they want you to believe in ghosts," she pointed to the third bedroom. "They know you are going to redecorate that hideous room."

"What!?" The shout came from the hideous room. "What did you say?"

Sally jumped up. She swayed as if she might fall. Maxine grabbed her and steadied her.

The hideous room had two doors. One next to the front door and one that opened to the kitchen next to the small dining room table in the kitchen.

Maxine and Sally stared at the door to their left and watched as the doorknob turned. The door opened slowly. The woman Maxine had seen in her dream stood there glaring at Maxine. She more or less looked like a living person . . . maybe less, in a shimmering, foggy kind of way.

Sally grabbed her round belly and whispered, "Oh, dear God."

Maxine ignored the rata-tat-tat of her own heart because the color had drained from Sally's face.

Her body suddenly looked like a rag doll as she sank to the floor.

Maxine kicked the chair away to clear the floor for Sally's fall.

As if it were happening in slow motion, Maxine realized the chair flew toward the sliding glass door next to the table, but her focus stayed on Sally. The ridiculous thought that this house had too many sliding glass doors popped into her mind as she grabbed her sister. One arm slid around her back and the other grabbed her ever-expanding waist.

Instantly, she realized that dead weight was heavier than the phrase sounded. Her arm muscles tightened as she lowered her sister safely to the ground.

Maxine fell to her knees and lifted Sally's head. She gently patted her cheek.

"Sally. Sally."

When Sally didn't instantly revive, Maxine shook her.

Should she call 911?

Could the baby be injured?

The old woman had stepped past them, and began rifling through the boxes on the countertop. She turned on the water and began soaking a dish towel.

Maxine didn't have time to think about ghosts or the fact that this crazy ghost was wetting a dish towel.

Instead, she gently shook Sally. Patted her cheeks and whispered, "Sally. Sally. Please, wake up."

"Stop that nonsense," the ghost said.

She tossed the wet towel, which Maxine grabbed without thinking.

"Wipe her face and neck, then put the cool tea towel on her wrists."

The ghost knelt down next to Sally and Maxine. "Don't they teach you girls anything nowadays?"

Annoyed at her interference, Maxine glared at her.

"Who are you? Florence Nightingale?"

"Oh, you're the funny one."

The ghost grabbed the dish towel, folded it, and laid it over Sally's forehead.

"I was a nurse. She just fainted. I didn't mean to frighten her. I didn't know she was with child."

Sally moaned and slowly opened her eyes. She focused on Maxine and turned her head toward the ghost.

Sally's eyes rolled upward.

The ghost very gently slapped her.

"Don't do that, girl. It's okay. No one is going to hurt you. Open your eyes."

Sally opened her eyes, they were rounder and bluer than Maxine had ever seen them.

"Very good," the ghost said in a very soothing voice. "Maxine and I are going to help you up and take you to that lovely sofa in the living room."

"You know my name?"

"Of course, I do. You've written it on everything

you own. Are you afraid of forgetting your own name? Now, be gentle. She's likely confused and anxious."

Maxine clamped her mouth shut to keep from saying, "And whose fault is that?"

3

Getting Sally to the sofa turned out to be relatively easy. She leaned on Maxine's arm. The ghost cleared a better pathway to the sofa. Instead of throwing things around, she picked up anything in the way, and placed the items neatly on top of boxes.

As they walked, Sally whispered, "Have we gone insane?"

"I can hear you," the ghost said.

"We know," Maxine said. "We aren't going to stop talking about you."

Not Florence Nightingale picked up a pillow that should have been on the tan chair that was now near the fireplace.

"Yes, of course. The ghost thing does take a while to get used to. Imagine my surprise when I woke up and realized I was dead."

She placed the pillow on the sofa.

"It took me two years to figure out how to become solid. Well, sort of solid. I have to warn you, I'll fade in a while. It's a lot of work, lifting things."

The not Florence Nightingale lowered Sally to the sofa and put her feet up. "Be a dear and lift her legs so I can put this pillow under her feet."

Maxine did has she told. Now that Sally seemed fine, she had a million questions for the ghost woman.

Maxine pulled a tan and green striped throw out of the box marked 'living room accessories' and put it over Sally. She sat on the floor beside her sister.

While Maxine watched Sally, her mind tried to deal with facts. First, not Florence Nightingale was definitely a ghost with a corporeal body. Second, two people who didn't believe in ghosts just simply accepted that she was a ghost. Third, this was some weird-ass shit.

What could be going on here? She could be a real woman who was tricking them so she could live in the house.

Maxine watched as Sally took the woman's hand. "Thank you so much. You've been so kind."

"Think nothing of it. If I'd realized you were with child, I wouldn't have said anything or materialized."

There was that "with child" phrase again. Just how old was this woman? ghost? spirt? whatever.

She was tall for a woman. Of course, Maxine had no way of knowing if she was tall for a ghost. No one knew what ghosts were supposed to be like.

This one had brown hair that she wore straight—about shoulder length. Her pants were bell-bottom pants. Not just any bell-bottoms, but the kind in old pictures of people in the 1970s. The bell part was so wide the fabric flopped around when she walked.

Come to think of it, she looked like someone who could have been at Woodstock. Of course, half the Baby Boomers she'd met claimed to have been at Woodstock, which, of course, was impossible. She assumed 98% of them were lying. They probably hated hippies when they were young, but now it was cooler to be an old hippy than it was to be just old and grouchy.

"Well, I'm so glad you did just step out of that room. It's delightful to have a nurse help me."

Okay, her sister was losing her everlasting mind.

"How far along are you? Is it a boy or a girl?"

"Almost seven months." Sally grinned. "A girl."

"Oh, girls are so wonderful. Less work than boys." The ghost glanced at Maxine. "Of course, that's not always true."

Maxine didn't take the bait.

"Sooo," Maxine purposefully exaggerated the word. "We need to talk."

Not Florence Nightingale smiled. "Of course, dear."

Maxine squinted at her. "Were you thinking of me as dear when you wrote on my wall?"

"No, I was not. I wanted to talk to you, and since you were letting Tibbs sleep with you . . ." she shrugged. " . . . I thought maybe you were nicer than the other people. I wanted to make a deal. And you were rude."

"I was asleep after a very long day of moving. I . . . needed . . . to . . . sleep."

Sally glared at Maxine with her eyes wide. A clear big sister look that said, "Be nice."

"Yes, you are perfectly right. I do apologize. I was so happy to be free from that witch's spell that I overstepped propriety."

"Overstepped propriety" . . . how old was this ghost?

"Witch? Literal witch or figurative expression?" Sally said, glancing from the ghost to Maxine.

The ghost pulled one of the larger boxes closer to the sofa and sat on it. Thankfully, Maxine didn't see any indentation.

"Well, literal. She placed a spell on that horrid room with that ridiculous furniture. I couldn't leave the room until Maxine and the rest of you arrived. Then suddenly I could leave the room."

Maxine looked at Sally. "Pinch me. Hard."

"No."

"Yes."

The ghost hopped up and grabbed Maxine's arm and pinched it.

"Ouch."

"You wanted to know if you were dreaming, right?"

Maxine rubbed her arm and nodded.

"If you can believe in me, then believe in the witch. She's truly evil."

During their exchange Sally had fallen asleep. Not Florence Nightingale put the index finger to her lips and motioned Maxine to follow her. They tiptoed into the kitchen and sat at the kitchen table.

Maxine considered the ghost and wondered how they could make the best of this situation. She wasn't certain that she believed in the witch, but at this point anything was possible.

She pulled another bear claw out of the white sack and considered the ghost. She held out the pastry.

"Do you eat?"

"No, thank you."

Maxine bit into the bear claw and savored the sugary taste.

"So, what's your name? What did you want to tell me last night? I'm Maxine. Most people call me Max. Since we are going to be roomies, call me Max."

Not Florence Nightingale smiled. "I'm Roxy, not my real name, which is Roberta Alma Jacobs. I used to throw rocks as a child, and some snot-nosed kid called me that and it stuck. Roxy works."

Maxine took another bite and waited for Roxy to continue.

"Here is the sad story. I died. I woke up standing in a graveyard. I thought I was alive and disoriented." She shrugged. "I went to a party, accidentally took some drugs. It was the seventies. Things happened. Apparently, I died. I wandered around for a while. Came here where my grandparents lived. Everything was fine until they died. Raven the Witch moved in with her freaky boyfriend slash husband."

Roxy stood up and moved to the window.

"Max, come look."

Maxine came and stared out at the half dead grass. "My grandfather was a landscape architect. He taught me everything. I helped him turn this yard into a lovely garden."

"That sounds wonderful. Did you have a vegetable garden, too?"

She nodded. "Yes. See the old neglected trees. One is an orange, one is a lemon, and the one they chopped down was an avocado."

"Who lived here after your grandparents?"

"My aunt . . . we got along. She died some years ago. Then along came Raven." She turned away from the window. "Truthfully, we tortured each other until I finally ran them off."

They turned from the window to find Sally standing in the doorway. Her hair was a little messy, but otherwise she looked refreshed, and her smile was wide.

"Come here," she said.

Sally placed Maxine's hand on her round belly. After a few seconds, there was a little knot pressing her skin forward. Then in rapid succession there were three more.

Maxine chuckled.

Sally waved Roxy over and did the same with her hand. A few seconds later Roxy smiled too.

A few minutes later, Maxine and Sally sat on the

sofa while Roxy, paced back and forth between the sofa and the front door. Finally, she spoke.

"I would very much like to stay here. You can do whatever you want with that horrible room. I don't need my own room. If it's all right, I would like to turn the yard back into a garden paradise. Tibbs isn't real. Raven thinks she invented him when she cast a spell. He was a figment of her imagination. I made horrible sounds pretending to be Tibbs. I did it to pay her back for locking me in that room. Sprinkles is real. He's a nice stray cat that wandered into the yard. Think about it. Let me stay and work in the yard."

Roxy's body faded.

Sally grabbed Maxine's hand and squeezed it.

"This may be the strangest day I've ever had," she said.

"I agree." Maxine looked at the spot where Roxy had been pacing. "She died in the seventies from an overdose."

Sally stood up. "It's none of my business, but I think you should consider her proposal. Just think, you'd have a free gardener and a nurse."

"I heard that," Roxy called from the kitchen.

## 4

Two years after Maxine moved into her house, she came home to find a white and tan kitten sitting on the front porch. Beside him, Roxy in her corporeal form sipped tea and petted the cat. She wore a sundress made of tie-dyed green and yellow fabric.

She smiled as Maxine took a very large box from the backseat. The wrapping paper had ballerinas dancing and on top of the box sat a huge purple bow.

The red leaves of the Japanese maple in the front yard sparkled with water drops as the sprinklers turned off. Last month, a picture of the front yard appeared in the local magazine with an article on drought tolerant plants.

Sally opened the front door, and stepped onto the porch carrying Teresa on her hip. The child had a riot of long curly red hair, just like her father.

Their brother, Philip, wearing a red-striped apron and carrying a very large spatula, followed Sally outside.

"The barbecue is hot," he called out. "I hope you're ready to party. We have a birthday to celebrate."

Teresa clapped her hands. "Birthday. Kitty."

"Ice and sodas are in the trunk," Maxine called out.

They all trooped to the backyard, where the aroma of barbecued hamburgers filled the air. A red checkered tablecloth covered the picnic table, colorful balloons attached to the patio bobbed in the breeze, and a small pile of gifts waited for Teresa to open them.

Teresa sat on the bench, patted the wooden seat with her chubby hand, and said, "Auntie Roxy."

That night when everything had been cleaned up, Roxy and Maxine sat on the sofa watching TV. Sprinkles and the new kitten, Stinky, were curled up between them. Roxy reached over and tapped Maxine's arm.

"It's about two years too late, but thank you."

Maxine smiled, knowing they had all benefited from having Roxy as part of their lives.

# CORA FOERSTNER

Author of the Dragon Speakers Duology

*you might
be depressed too
if you woke up
dead*

## Lucas Maxwell

A Spooky Short Story

## LUCAS MAXWELL: A DECENT MAN

### BECOMING: A GHOST'S LIFE

Lucas Maxwell wasn't sure how long he'd been a ghost. Becoming a ghost was sorta like coming out of anesthesia after surgery.

You wake up. You're confused for awhile, expecting to understand where you are—like waking up in a strange motel room and it takes a few moments to remember where you are.

The problem with understanding is you're either in a coffin or in a cemetery. In Lucas' case, he was standing in a cemetery right on his in-ground slab with his name written on it.

There wasn't a way to keep track of time. So was he in some kind of limbo for years or had only a short amount of time passed? He didn't know.

At first, after he realized he was a ghost, he'd just sat beside his stone plaque on the ground and looked at the trees, the sky, and the animals.

There were wild blackberries all over the cemetery. So birds, squirrels, raccoons, and even sometimes bobcats wandered through. He wasn't sure if bobcats ate berries, but they might.

The cemetery was so quiet that even the smallest disturbance was a distraction.

He figured out he was dead when he discovered the plaque and read it.

*Lucas Maxwell, beloved partner,*
*the most decent man*
*on the face of the earth.*

He knew Candy had written those words for him. She used to always say, "You're the most decent man on the face of the earth," and when she was angry, she'd say, "Just like a vampire, you're sucking the life out of me."

When Lucas asked her to marry him, she flat out said, "No, are you trying to suck the life out of me?"

From that point onward he decided to never speak of marriage again. She definitely equated marriage with death.

He'd always laughed her drama off. She was a drag queen, and she loved drama. That was one of the things that made him fall in love with her. She dressed in wild colors. He thought of her dancing through life wearing primary colors and lifting her arms to the sky.

One spring day in the cemetery, when the grass was like velvet and dandelions dotted the lawn, he sat down on the dew-soaked grass. He didn't know for sure, but he guessed the air was chilly. He watched the clouds slowly slink by and tried to figure out what had happened to him.

He couldn't remember anything about his death.

That day, his friend, Jeff from work, and Jeff's wife came walking by him. They both wore jackets proving his theory about the weather correct. They didn't notice him. More likely than not noticing, they couldn't see him.

They were one of those couples who looked like each other. They were tall, lanky, with brown hair and blue eyes. Other than physical appearance, they were nothing alike.

She chatted all the time, and Jeff rarely spoke in

complete sentences. He often nodded or spoke with a series of one-syllable words like "Yeah," or "Sure," or "Right," or "Maybe."

They stopped and looked right at him, not seeing him.

"Poor Lucas," Jeff said, "a decent guy."

"Well it's a sad, sad story. Poor, poor man. His crazy boyfriend poisoned him and is rotting away in prison. That's where he belongs. That's what I said. What's that popular saying?"

"Don't know," Jeff said.

"Oh, yeah, fuck around and find out."

"That doesn't apply here. Someone killed him," Jeff said.

Lucas almost teared up. Jeff sounded outraged, defending him, and sad about his death.

"It applies. His partner killed him."

"But I can tell you for sure that Candy didn't poison him. They loved each other."

L ucas was pretty sure Jeff's wife didn't catch the frown he gave her when she was badmouthing Candy, 'cause she just kept on talking and talking.

Their words finally sank deep down into Lucas' heart. He bolted up off the grass.

"Jeff! Jeff!"

No matter how loud he shouted, Jeff didn't hear or see him. He jumped down in front of them, shouted, and waved his arms.

He did everything he could to get them to see him.

That day being a ghost turned from, "Okay, I'm dead. I can deal with this" to "Help! Help! Candy didn't kill me."

He didn't remember what happened, but he knew, without knowing how he knew, that Candy did not kill him.

After that day, all he could think about was Candy.

His death put her in jail. Indirectly, he really did suck the life out of her. A drag queen in prison had to be far worse than being a ghost.

That day he started keeping track of the days. He used a stick to make marks on one of the older gravestones in the cemetery. The cement was weathered, and he could scratch a mark into the stone.

He had almost a year's worth of marks on the back of the stone, when an older woman with gray hair pulled into a bun came and stood at the grave. Quiet tears slid down her wrinkled cheeks. She placed a dozen yellow roses on JP Wooster's grave.

When she saw Lucas' stick marks, she began mumbling, saying that someone had defaced her husband's gravestone. She must have complained to the caretaker because the old man with bent shoulders made the long trek from the gatehouse to the middle of the cemetery.

The old man ignored the freak snow falling, the cold, and worked a little bit every day to fix the gravestone for that old woman. It didn't take him too long to rub out all the marks.

But Luvas felt small and guilty for not considering how what he did affected other people.

He'd had a habit of doing that when he was alive. If he'd been more considerate, maybe Candy wouldn't have thought he was sucking the life out of her.

Every day, he found himself saying, "I sucked the life out of her. I sucked the life out of her. It's all my fault."

He remembered when he was younger, his older sister used to say about one of her boyfriends, "He's a vampire. He sucks the life out of me."

He'd become a vampire, and he hadn't even realized that he'd made the transition. Now he wasn't just lonely, he was going crazy.

All he thought about was Candy in prison. He doubted the people in prison were kind to her. He had caused her life to become a living hell.

Day and night he went over and over what had happened before he died. He tried to figure out how he was poisoned.

He lived on a cul-de-sac. Everyone on the block was friendly and nice, except for Mrs. Freeman who liked to gossip. Over the years her meddling had caused a few problems—she disliked teenagers.

All the homes were well cared for and in perfect order. Except for Mr. Crispin's house. He didn't always keep his yard up.

Then out of the blue, Lucas remembered one very, very important thing.


THE PAST: DOES IT MATTER?

Jennifer Williamson was Lucas and Candy's next-door neighbor. She, Candy, and Lucas were besties. Jen used to call them the three musketeers.

His memories of the three of them meshed together like a giant collage of images, colors, sounds of laughter, and quiet moments of watching serious movies.

When he was alive, they had a good life. He remembered that Jen was funny, a good dancer, and a singer. Once Candy invited her to sing with her at one of her drag shows. Jen was too shy, but he could tell that she liked the compliments.

He thought the invite was odd because he couldn't imagine a woman among all the drag queens. He knew Candy brought it up to let Jen know she was a good singer. Later, he wished she'd said yes. He would have enjoyed that show, to see everyone's reaction.

In the summer, they barbecued, took weekend trips together, and once, when Jen and her ex were trying to get back together, Carl joined them. Within hours everyone knew why she'd divorced the guy.

Candy dubbed him Mr. Downer Guy.

After that outing, Candy told Jen that she deserved better. She must have taken those words to heart because shortly after, Mr. Downer Guy quit coming around.

A few months later, Jen announced that Mr. Downer Guyhad remarried.

"That's all right girl, you got us," Candy said.

Jen smiled and looked at Candy the way someone looks at the love of their life. The expression was just a little flash . . .admiration, softness, and complete and utter lust.

In that moment, Lucas wondered if Jen knew how she felt and if Candy knew how Jen felt.

That night, Candy had undressed and was sitting at her makeup table taking off layers of eye shadow, when Lucas took the opportunity to bring the subject up.

"I think we have a love triangle problem," Lucas said.

Candy laughed.

"Is Abby flirting with you again?" She watched Lucas in the mirror as she picked up her night cream.

Lucas shook his head. Their gazes met in the mirror. Candy's blue eyes widened as she smiled.

"Today, I saw Jen give you that universal look of lust and love or maybe just love."

Candy put the jar of cream down and turned to face him. She sighed.

"Babe, I saw the same look. I promise." She used her index finger to paint an invisible cross over her heart. "Nothing, I mean, zero, zip has happened."

Lucas sat on the edge of the bed, and looked at Candy without her wig or her makeup or her flashy dresses, and realized he loved her with his whole heart.

"She's so broken," Candy said.

"I know."

"What do we do?"

"Well, . . ." Lucas remembered that long pause as he considered the question. The silence was the loudest quiet he'd ever heard. "She might not know."

That was all he had.

"Or she does know. She's a little sneaky about it, but she knows. So, do we carry on as if we didn't notice? Or do we slowly pull back?" Candy's blue eyes seemed to be like laser points as she watched him.

"Let's carry on. I doubt she'd ever say anything. Maybe we should start finding her blind dates. Maybe she will find someone else. We are her only friends."

The first raindrop that fell on Lucas's nose

brought him back to the present. It wasn't long until rain dripped off him in little rivulets. He hated when it rained. He knew he didn't need shelter, but it would have been nice.

Now as raindrops pelted his head, he considered and wondered if they had done the right thing.

He headed to the tall pine tree in the corner nearest him. There he sat in the dirt under the tree's canopy. He glanced up at the dark gray clouds moving through the sky.

A hummingbird darted close to his face and darted away toward a rose bush that grew against the stone fence. He wasn't the only one looking for shelter.

Even in hindsight, he couldn't decide. He missed Candy. Was he a vampire? Did he drive her crazy? Sometimes he said yes to those questions and other times he said no. Candy was expressive, flamboyant, and loved hyperbole. She'd simply been being herself when she said he was sucking the life out of her or did she mean it?

The questions were driving him crazy. He leaned against the tree's trunk and sighed.

He watched the rain for a long time and finally decided that he'd done the best he could and that might not have been enough. He'd never know.

What he did know was that no matter how much fun Candy, Jen, and he had had, no matter how much better Jen's life got, she still wallowed in sadness. Lucas wondered if she were one of those people who needed constant reassurances or constant companionship.

After meeting the ex-husband who would make Attila the Hun look like a peaceful guy, Candy went out of her way to invite Jen to their get-togethers.

On Jen's thirty-second birthday, Candy threw a cul-de-sac party.

It was early June, all the yards were blooming. Old Mr. Hatch had four different blooming trees in his yard at the end of the cul-de-sac. His place was ablaze with reds, yellows, pinks, and whites.

Candy set up tables in his driveway. She put balloons on all the non-blooming trees. There was a long table for the neighborhood kids. Lucas was certain there were extra kids from other blocks, but no one cared because everyone was having fun.

That was the day that Jen brought her carrot cake muffins to the party.

Lucas closed his eyes and imagined the first bite. Those muffins were heavenly. Even the angels would have oohed and aahed over them.

He held up his muffin, and said to everyone sitting at his table, "These muffins are to die for!"

Everyone agreed, but privately Candy told him she hated carrot cake and muffins. She must have told Jen too because not long after that, once or twice a week Jen started bringing them chocolate cupcakes and carrot cake muffins. Chocolate cupcakes were for Candy, and carrot cupcakes were for him.

Lucas laid back on the grass and glanced up at the clouds. Those were great memories, but they didn't help him figure out who could have poisoned him.

Unless . . . unless? Could it be?

Lucas got up. It had stopped raining. He walked across the cemetery and back. He kept walking. The green grass was wet, soggy, squishy, which wasn't at all surprising since it had just rained.

Well, it rained most of the time in Washington, but not as much as most people in other states thought. The trees were full of leaves, the squirrels were scampering up the trees. One even fussed at him as he walked past.

He assumed it was a mama squirrel who didn't want him to frighten her babies. He walked in circles, his shoes making splashing noises as he stepped in puddles. Lucas didn't care about bothering squirrels or messing up the grass or anything.

Dark clouds rolled across the sky, blocking the sun. The first raindrops started, slow at first then faster and bigger.

He couldn't stop walking or thinking, and thinking, and thinking.

The thinking started making him crazy. He didn't realize that he was going crazy until one day he ran into Sam, another ghost.

On his journey to crazyland, he'd seen other ghosts. A few were friendly until they began to avoid him, and then he noticed they were gone.

At one point, he remembered someone shouting at him, "Go to the light, dude. That light is for you. Go to the light."

He looked up and saw light. It was a big, long, blindingly bright light that went from the ground and jetted up into the sky.

There was a moment when he thought, "Yes, maybe it's beautiful and happy where the light goes."

But he couldn't go. Not when he knew the horrible, terrible, heartbreaking truth.

He had driven his partner crazy. Now he'd driven himself crazy. Over and over he heard himself say, "I drove her crazy. I drove her crazy. I'm a vampire. I suck the life out of everyone. No one is safe around me. I suck the life out of everyone. I'm a vampire."

He realized he had become one of those people that everyone would avoid. Well, he'd driven the other ghosts away with his constant questioning or they had all gone into the light. He'd missed his opportunity to go.


## SAM: FIFTY MILES

After spending a long time talking to himself and trying to figure out what had happened to Candy, he found himself alone.

Then Sam was there, standing in front of him. He was tall, broad-shouldered, and scruffy-looking. One of those men who had a quarter inch of beard five minutes after they shaved. His black hair was pulled back in a pony tail. He looked about fifty, but Lucas guessed he was probably forty-ish. A forty-something with fifty miles of bad road at his back.

Of course, everything about him was grayish and wispy. Like all the ghosts Lucas had seen, Sam had the same look. Ghosts looked like smoke. The kind that a light breeze would blow away as it vanished in the distance.

He stood there and stared at Lucas. He wasn't exactly frowning, but he definitely wasn't smiling. He could have been on the verge of annoyance.

"Man, what are you doing?" Sam said.

Lucas glanced around. Yeah, he was the only one around, and Sam wasn't backing away.

Lucas shrugged. "Nothing. I'm not doing anything."

"You're disturbing the calm of the entire cemetery."

To be truthful, Lucas had no idea what this man was talking about. Everything here was calm, boringly calm. Nothing ever happened. Birds might come by and steal a few berries, the wind blew the leaves on the trees, an old lady complained about gravestones, and the caretaker fixed things. Only funeral goers made noise, and they mostly wept quietly. Occasionally, there was a loud distraught person, but mostly quiet and whispers.

He didn't think he liked this guy.

"Listen, my name is Sam." He held out his hand.

Well, damn, he said that so nice that Lucas couldn't exactly shout at him and tell him to mind his own business or to go back to his side of the cemetery.

"Lucas," he said, and shook Sam's hand.

"Lucas, I've been watching you and listening to your wailing and moaning—"

"I don't wail and moan."

"Yes, you do. You wail. Then you say, 'I sucked the life out of her,' and every once in a while you say, 'I'm a vampire. I suck the life out of people.'"

Lucas considered the man for a moment. He hadn't raised his voice. What he said was true. He didn't sound angry like the other ghosts who kept shouting for him to "shut up".

"I do suck the life out of people. I am a vampire."

Sam shook his head.

"No, you're not a vampire. Vampires aren't real."

"A lot of people believe ghosts aren't real, yet here we are."

"Here's the deal. I think you need a friend. Someone to talk to so you aren't alone. Vampires aren't real, which I think you know. I also think if you have something to do besides go over and over about what happened to you, you'd feel better."

The guy made sense. Having a friend might get his mind off Candy.

"What makes you think I'm going over what happened to me?"

Sam shrugged his big buff shoulders.

"Because I did the same thing when I woke up

dead." He spread his arms wide. "Right here in this cemetery."

"You want to be my friend? Why?"

He nodded. "I do. Pay it forward."

"What are you plying forward?"

"Someone helped me adjust. I thought maybe I could help you."

So things changed for the better. Sam let Lucas talk about Candy and what may or may not have happened to him. Sam talked about everything. He called himself a self-educated man. He particularly liked philosophy and history.

Every day Lucas got a little better. He said, "I sucked the life out of her" a lot less. He admitted that the vampire claim was a metaphor for what he thought he'd done.

One thing that Lucas couldn't let go of was that Candy was in prison. It plagued him. Whenever he thought about it too much, he'd fall back into his old ways.

One evening he and Sam were discussing Marcus Aurelius. Lucas listened, amazed that Sam could quote long portions from Marcus Aurelius' *Meditations*. Lucas loved to listen to Sam because his voice was soothing and calm. What surprised him the most was that an emperor who lived hundreds of years ago tried to be a good man.

Every day, he tried. He even admitted that me made mistakes. Lucas liked that.

"I'm impressed that one of the greatest Roman emperors was a man who tried to do the right thing. I think someone with that much power and responsibility might care about money, pleasures, and power more than anything else. I'm not sure we have leaders like that now."

Sam looked up at the moon. "You may be right. Aurelius was a rare leader. I like to think there are still a few people all over the world who try."

"Sam, do you ever wish you had lived longer?"

Sam grinned. Now that Lucas knew him better, he knew that the man before him was a serious man, someone who rarely laughed but often smiled. He was the opposite of Candy, who laughed, smiled, sang, and lived every day to its fullest.

"I do," Sam said. "I think we all do. If you are going to ask me what I'd do if I were alive, don't. I'll never answer that question."

"Too bad," Lucas said. "That is what I was going to ask."

"I don't have to ask you that question. I know what

you'd do. I read your gravestone. Candy said you were the most decent man she'd ever known. I think I agree with her. I also think that's why you are caught in a loop trying to answer questions you know the answer to."

Lucas looked at Sam and shook his head. He knew the man would claim that he was shaking his head denying what Sam had said. He wasn't rejecting the compliment, but he really didn't know who poisoned him. He just knew Candy didn't do it.

Maybe he was a decent man. That was a good thing.

"I don't know the answers to the questions I'm asking myself."

Sam had been sitting on the stone fence that bordered the cemetery. He jumped off and dusted off his pants. There was nothing there. Only imaginary dust or dampness.

The breeze shook the leaves of the weeping birch beside them. Sometimes Lucas thought it would be nice to feel the breeze or the cold snowflakes landing on his face.

"Look at that moon. There's something wonderful about a full moon," Sam said.

Lucas didn't answer because he knew it was a rhetorical question and that Sam wanted to tell him something.

"You know you're a decent man, don't you, Lucas."

"Yes."

"You're a decent man who loves Candy. You agonize over her plight, and you blame yourself."

Lucas kept his eyes on the full moon. "Yes, that's right."

Sam silently looked down at the ground. The seconds ticked by, and Lucas waited for his friend to make his point.

"You also love Jen in a neighborly way. What's the hardest thing for a decent man to reconcile when he loves two people?"

Lucas swallowed and pondered the question. This wasn't like the times he wandered the cemetery agonizing in the pain of Candy's imprisonment and the question of who poisoned him. This was about the truth he'd been avoiding since Jeff and his wife accidentally told him that Candy was in prison for murdering him.

The answer was simple. If you love someone, you never want to believe that they'd purposefully hurt you. So he couldn't face the truth because it was too hard to believe.

Lucas didn't answer him.

Together they waited in the night's silence and stared at the moon.

"Why do you think she did it?" Sam asked.

Lucas glanced at Sam. He could see the gray hairs in his stubble of a beard. He sighed.

"I think she didn't realize that Candy loved hyperbole. She truly, honestly thought my Candy was unhappy."

Sam nodded. He turned his head and looked right in Lucas' eyes.

"If I were alive," Sam said. "I'd try to be a decent man."

# CORA FOERSTNER

Author of the Dragon Speakers Duology



# Haunted Cabin

A Spooky Short Story

4

HAUNTED CABIN

After driving two hours up the San Bernardino Mountains in Southern California, Marci wished she had taken Janet up on her offer to ride share. It wasn't that there were bad road conditions. Traffic. Yeah, Southern California always meant there was a possibility of bad traffic. She had been naive enough to think driving up to the mountains for a quiet weekend would be different.

Traffic had slowed to a crawl even before she started up the mountain. What she didn't do was check the weather. Apparently, the possibility of snow was the magic that created the traffic jam. If she'd been with Janet, they would have entertained each other.

This morning the sun shone bright and warm.

The clear blue sky remained cloudless. Her brother, who didn't like the idea of her driving up to Big Bear alone, had made her put chains in her car.

Like she'd know what to do with them. She kept her mouth closed and tossed them in the trunk.

"Just in case," he said and frowned. "Be careful."

She had rolled her eyes.

"Be careful of people. People go up there to party. It'll be crowded. There will be drinking and drugs. People will be crazy."

She loved her brother, but at twenty-four, he sounded as if he were an eighty-four year old man. When he got older, he was going to be the neighborhood grouch.

When she finally drove past the cute town of Big Bear, she wistfully glanced over at Big Bear Lake. She'd wanted to stay by the lake, but her friends vetoed that in favor of a cabin in the forest.

She took so many turns and twists that when her car's GPS finally said, "You have arrived at your destination," she literally said, "Hallelujah."

She parked in front of an actual log cabin. It wasn't exactly run-down, but it was old and not the image online that advertised "for a perfect relaxing vacation." This was not the kind of place for the wild parties her brother predicted.

For a moment, she thought this was the wrong place, but Janet's green Ford Focus was parked in the driveway.

The cabin was deep into the forest area and surrounded by tall pine trees. About a half mile back she'd taken a right turn off the paved road to a narrow dirt road. So this was definitely wilderness.

Bummer. There was no grass around the cabin. No lake. Probably nothing fun to do.

Mike had parked his Honda Fit at an angle so it squeezed into the space between Janet's Focus and a huge pine tree.

Marci smiled as she grabbed her suitcase from the trunk. Mike hated the Fit. It had been his mother's car. He was six feet, four inches tall. Watching him fold himself into the car entertained her immensely.

Janet once told her that he parked in dangerous locations hoping someone would hit the car and total it. Yes, that was a crazy way to get a new car, but Mike was a little crazy. She seriously doubted a pine tree would suddenly fall on his car.

The cabin door flew open.

"Marci!"

Janet skipped out of the cabin looking like a little girl. Her jet black hair was pulled up in pigtails. Her jeans had holes in the legs, and she wore a navy tank top. Marci could see goosebumps on her arms.

Janet's body never seemed to get the "it's chilly outside" message. She came to college from Wisconsin because she never wanted to see snow again. Even in December in Southern California, the weather was chilly and could turn cold as soon as the sun went down.

"Need help?" Janet said. "The cabin's sorta creepy. Too bad it's not Halloween."

"Soda in the trunk. Potato salad and roast in the ice chest," Marci said as she lifted her suitcase and started toward the cabin. "Don't ask about the roast. We can slice it for sandwiches. My mom insisted on sending it. Did Sam come with Mike?"

Janet pulled the soda and ice chest out of the trunk and slammed the trunk down hard. Marci ignored the charging-bull approach her friend had toward simple actions.

Her grandmother would have said she was born in a barn. Marci never really got the meaning of the saying. She assumed it was something old people said to dump on young people. Or that people born in a barn were animals. Probably the latter, but she'd never admit to her grandmother that she knew the meaning.

"Yeah. Sam said Mike cursed all the way here." She chuckled. "They are super mad about the cabin. They went out exploring. And . . . the cabin isn't livable. You'll see."

Somehow Janet's voice made "the cabin isn't livable" sound like an adventure. Inside, Marci plopped her suitcase down on the grimy floor. When the suitcase landed, dust spewed a rotting fragrance into the air.

Marci glanced around. They'd rented a two bedroom cabin. This was one very small room.

The "kitchen" held a ruggedly made cabinet that looked like a workbench from an old garage. In the corner a large bucket sat on the floor under an rusted water pump. If this was a fully equipped kitchen, she was a billionaire from Carmel. No bathroom or the promised bedrooms. Great . . . what other delights awaited them?

There were holes, gaping holes, where the plaster between the logs should have been. Whatever had been there previously had deteriorated. Sunlight came filtered into the cabin and highlighted the grime on the floor.

Maybe the guys went out looking for mud to fill the holes.

The furniture consisted of two tan chairs of

dubious condition and a love seat covered in dust and fallen leaves. It also sagged in the center.

Marci glanced up. There was a jagged hole right over the sofa. Dried leaves were caught on the pointed parts of the wood.

Sorta creepy really didn't do justice to the despicable condition of the cabin.

Behind her Janet dropped the ice chest on the floor. Her hands went right to her hips, her mouth turned down into a perfect imitation of a sad smiley face.

"We cannot stay here," Marci said.

"No shit."

"Where did the guys really go?"

"They are hiking around looking for bars."

"Bars? They are drinking while we are standing here in this filth."

"Our phones aren't working. Mike said they needed bars."Janet shrugged.

"That's not a thing anymore. Phone service bounces off cellular stations and satellites. I don't know the details, but bars are something our parents say."

"Don't ask me. Mike said something here was blocking the phones. He claimed, if they got away from the cabin, they could call the people who rented us this pile of junk."

Ten minutes later they were sitting on the steps that led to the cabin, waiting for Mike and Sam. Janet had pulled a hoodie out of her suitcase and slipped it on.

If Janet felt the cold, that meant the weather was definitely getting chillier. Marci tried her phone again. No cell signal. She walked away from the cabin, holding her phone up. She went in every direction. Nothing.

She walked back toward the cabin. Just inside the cabin door, a shrouded figure that looked like he was surrounded by a haze stood behind Janet.

Adrenaline shot through Marci's body. Her heart raced and her body became seriously alert. Her instinct was to shout, but that would frighten Janet.

Instead, she raced forward, running as if she were doing the hundred yard dash. The man or person standing behind her friend stood there still and quiet. He hadn't moved. His eyes glowed yellow as he watched her run.

Just before she reached the steps where Janet sat, she skidded to a stop.

She grabbed her friend's arm and yanked her up. She pulled a reluctant Janet along with her.

"Run!"

"What are you doing!"

When they were almost to the trees, Marci stopped.

She panted, trying to catch her breath. Janet yanked her arm away. She glared at Marci as she rubbed her arm.

"Are you crazy?"

Marci didn't answer, she pointed toward the cabin. The shrouded figure was still there in the shadows.

Janet squinted and wrinkled her forehead. Then she reached in her jeans' pocket and pulled out her glasses.

As soon as she put them on, she jumped back. "Holy shit, who's that? What is that?"

"Someone is trying to scare us. Is there a door or opening in the back of the cabin? Could Mike or Sam get in?"

Janet stared at the person in the doorway and swallowed. "No, nothing. You know our stuff is in there."

There were a lot of things that Marci knew. First she knew they needed to get to their cars and leave. Second, as Janet observed, their stuff, including keys, was in the cabin.

"Do you happen to have your car keys?' Marci whispered.

She wasn't sure why she was whispering. It just seemed like this was one of those weird situations where whispering was necessary.

"No, besides, you're parked behind me."

They were in some sort of standoff. That person was about as tall as Sam. It definitely wasn't Mike. For Halloween Sam'd dressed up in a black robe and wore a creepy mask. He probably sneaked inside while she and Janet were getting stuff out of the car.

"It's Sam," Marci said.

"If it's Sam, I'm going to kill him. Why are we just standing here? His eyes are glowing. How is that possible?"

"A mask. Let's grab a fallen branch and use it as a weapon. We are going to run at the house and beat him with the branch. Don't get one that's too heavy. We don't want to hurt him."

Janet grabbed the branch closest to her. She swung it like a bat a few times.

"I want to hurt him. My heart is still trying to beat its way out of my chest. Plus, now I have to pee. I'm not going to do that in these woods."

Marci stared at the figure. With all their talking, moving around, and swinging branches, he never moved. It suddenly occurred to her that if that was Sam, where was Mike? It didn't matter. He was probably hiding in the bushes laughing at them.

"On three, we run and pound him," Marci said.

Janet nodded.

"1 . . . 2 . . .3!"

Marci sprinted forward watching Sam, who still hadn't moved.

Beside her Janet shouted, "You're gonna regret this."

They were about ten feet from the steps when Mike and Sam walked out of the woods near the parked cars.

In a fraction of a second, Marci realized the thing was still in the doorway and the guys were coming back from their walkabout.

Mike and Sam stopped and stared as Marci ran past.

She was going too fast to stop. She realized that they were about to attack a stranger, who could very well be extremely dangerous. She was running too fast.

Janet went through the door first. The man didn't move, and Janet ran right through him like he was nothing but a puff of smoke.

Marci tried to skid to a stop, but it didn't work.

She followed Janet into the house. Inside the doorway, she hit a freezing haze that scooted away from her. Cold, a deep bone-chilling cold like someone pouring icy water over her whole body hit her. Marci yelled a cry of freezing anguish.

Her momentum propelled her forward and into Janet. They both fell to the floor, stirring up dust, making the air smell like musty dried leaves and moss.

Coughing the toxins out of her lungs, Marci pulled Janet to her feet. Janet was still holding her branch, which whacked Marci in the leg.

"Ouch." She reached down and checked her leg for cuts or welts. Nothing.

She scanned the room. The man or the thing stood in the corner. Her fear became a knot in her throat. She grabbed Janet's tank top and dragged her back toward the door and outside. Mike and Sam stood a few feet from the cabin staring at them.

"What are you staring at?" Janet shouted.

When Sam laughed, she hit him in the ass with the branch she still carried.

Marci went up the three steps and glared inside. In the corner, the man or creature or whatever stared at her. Its yellow eyes were still shiny. He didn't move or try to rush past her. The cabin was colder, but that could probably be because the sun was going down.

It was colder. Her arms were icy cold. She had hurt her hand when she fell on the floor. Plus there was a rather large splinter in the palm of her hand. Her first thought was bacteria. Her second was they had to leave this place.

She stepped outside again.

"Get in there!"

Mike and Sam didn't move.

"Have you two lost your minds?" Mike asked.

When a huge snowflake landed on Marci's cheek, she realized it was snowing. The flakes were coming down fast. So fast everything looked fuzzy. In the few seconds she'd been inside, the snow was already sticking to the ground.

Mike and Sam stood on either side of Janet, who held each man's arm, pulling them close to her.

"So?" Mike's deep voice echoed in the small clearing.

"She told you?"

Sam and Mike nodded.

"He's still in there. It's wearing a creepy cape thing. Its eyes shine like a yellow light. I think it's a mask."

"It's a ghost," Janet said. "I ran right through it. It was freezing cold."

As if they'd planned it, the three of them took a step back.

"It's not a ghost. It's a man with a mask," Marci said, realizing she'd run right through him too. There had to be a sane explanation of how that happened.

Maybe it was a hologram? Maybe he was a ghost? She wasn't going to admit that. She planned to bully Sam and Mike to go inside and get their things.

"Here's the deal. It's snowing. We need our stuff. You two are going to go in and bring everything out."

Mike and Sam both shook their heads.

Marci squinted at them. "Cowards," she said as she stepped toward the cabin.

If there was ever a time when girl power worked, it was then. In her experience, no man wanted to be called a coward and then have a woman go do what he was afraid to do.

Her ploy worked.

Sam and Mike agreed. Laughed and claimed they wanted to see the ghost.

Before either man moved, a giant brown and

black German shepherd raced into the yard, barking and growling and barking some more.

The dog stopped about three feet from them and growled, showing his sharp teeth. A giant man, much taller and broader than Mike walked into the clearing. He had a full red beard and hair to match. His big heavy jacket was something Marci would have liked to rip off him and steal it.

"Brutus, sit and stop barking," the man said.

The dog whined and sat quietly.

"What are you folks doing here?"

Marci realized this man had nothing to do with their problems, but she was too frustrated to think properly.

She rushed forward. He could be trouble or he might help them.

Up close, he looked even bigger. Her head reached his chest. Slowly she looked up from the red and black plaid jacket into blue eyes and a friendly smile.

"We are a little freaked out," she said as she pointed back toward the cabin.

"You've seen the ghost?"

"Yes," Janet said. "I told you it was a ghost."

"You all should know better than coming up here and horsing around."

"Hey, wait a second. We weren't horsing around. We rented that junky cabin," Sam said.

"No," Mike said. "We didn't rent that. We were told it had two bedrooms, a kitchen, and a fireplace. Then we couldn't use our phones. We came back here to find them terrified."

"Wait. We weren't terrified," Marci said, pointing at the cabin again. "We were trying to fight that thing."

"You were screaming like banshees," Mike said.

Brutus sat next to his owner. The dog looked at Mike when he spoke and then back at his owner.

If Marci hadn't been freaked out of her mind, she would have thought the dog was adorable.

"All of you, be quiet," the man said.

In her mind, Marci had been calling him Johnny Appleseed. He just needed an axe to make the image perfect. Of course, if he'd come through the forest with an ax, she might have run away screaming.

No one spoke.

"Good. I take it that you aren't from around here."

Marci nodded.

"So someone ripped you off. This is the Allard's cabin. Been empty for a long time because it's haunted."

Marci opened her mouth.

The man held up his hand in the perfect STOP gesture.

"I know the ghost is still in there. He lives there. Who rented this place to you."

Sam pulled out his phone. "Holden & Sons Rentals."

"Umm, the Holdens are reputable. What address did they give you?"

Sam handed him his phone. Johnny Appleseed scanned the receipt Holden & Sons sent. He pressed his lips together and shook his head. He chuckled and shook his head some more.

"You folks are on the wrong side of the lake. You can follow me, and I'll get you headed in the right direction."

When Johnny Appleseed left to get his vehicle, Marci insisted that Sam and Mike get their supplies out of the cabin.

They returned laughing and talking.

"There wasn't a ghost in there," Mike said.

"You guys were tying to pull a fast one."

While the guys carried their supplies out of the cabin, Johnny Appleseed returned with his red truck. He waved Janet and Marci over.

Marci glanced back at the cabin. The ghost stood

in the door again. It glanced back inside the cabin and moved. A second later, Mike and Sam walked through the door.

She pointed to the doorway. They glanced behind them. Mike laughed.

"Not funny," he said, as he carried Marci's suitcase and placed it in her trunk.

Johnny Appleseed got back in his truck, and Marci called out to Mike and Sam. "We're following him."

They formed a caravan and within half an hour they found themselves in a modern cabin, with two bedrooms, a real bathroom, a kitchenette, electricity, a TV, and WiFi.

After showers and a change of clothes, they ate sandwiches, and rehashed their day's adventures.

"Marci, are you still seeing him?" Sam asked.

"Yeah. He's in that corner." She pointed to the corner, near the tan and white striped chair where Sam had been sitting just before they sat down to eat.

"Why didn't you tell me before?" Sam said, glancing into the corner.

Mike nodded. "I'm just glad we can't see him."

Janet stood and began clearing the paper plates and scraps of food. She stuffed them into a trash bag.

"You two are going to have to stay up while we sleep," Janet said as she grabbed a handful of chips.

"No way," Mike said. "I need my beauty sleep."

"We'll do it," Sam said.

"We will? Why?"

"Because I'm not sleeping here with that creepy thing staring at us. Even if I can't see him. He's here," he pointed at Mike. "You are staying up to keep me awake. He might kill us in our sleep."

Janet grabbed the trash bag and headed for the door. "I'm going to empty this."

"I'll go with you. It's dark outside," Mike said.

"Oh, now you are chivalrous. I'm fine. The creepy guy is in here."

Mike glanced into the corner. "Go away. We don't want you here."

Marci shook her head. "Still here." She stomped out of the cabin with the trash.

"Why's she mad?" Sam asked.

"Oh, I don't know. Maybe because you two left her in that cabin alone. Maybe because you laughed at us. Or hey, could it be that you sent us the wrong directions?"

Sam shrugged. "All true. I don't understand why we can't see him."

·  ·  ·

On a normal night, the bedroom would be nothing special, but after being in the woods in a haunted derelict cabin, this bedroom seemed marvelous. The gray and white bedspread was clean, the carpet was vacuumed, and there was a heater. It was still snowing outside.

Janet took the bed furthest from the door. Marci crawled into bed and remembered what Johnny Appleseed told them. She hopped up and went to the door.

She slipped into the living room. Sam and Mike were both sitting on the sofa, holding pillows close to their chests and staring at the ghost in the corner. The thought that she was getting used to his looks popped into her head. Maybe he was traumatized in life?

"Hey, guys," she said.

Mike squealed and Sam shouted "Holy hell, don't sneak up on us."

"Quit being babies. I thought I'd warn you, Johnny Appleseed said the reason we could see him was because at some point in the cabin we must have walked through the ghost. So be careful. If you feel something cold, stay away from that area or you'll start seeing him, too. Some people start seeing ghosts everywhere."

Sam's brown eyes squinted at her as he frowned.

On the other hand, Mike stuck his tongue out at her. "It would have been helpful if you'd told us that earlier."

Marci realized that Sam was sitting extremely close to Mike, not something they usually did. Also, they weren't using the pillows for resting. They both held their pillows to their chests and both had a sort of death grip to keep the pillows close.

Marci's little sister used to do that when she was scared.

"You can see him." Marci laughed.

Sam tossed his pillow at Marci. "He's terrifying. You could have told us about the cold and walking through him . . . you did this on purpose."

"He's harmless. He hasn't done anything," she said.

"That doesn't mean he won't," Mike said. "The ghost moved to the bathroom door. I walked in first and Sam followed when I yelped. I think he did that on purpose. He trapped us. Now he's going to haunt us forever."

Marci tried not to grin. She also refrained from saying the word "karma."

"Is he going to follow us everywhere? Will he be

at the university when we go back in January? Does he speak? What if he kills us?"

Mike stopped talking when he ran out of breath.

She walked to the sofa and sat between them.

"No to all your questions. He will only follow us while we are here."

The shrouded ghost stepped toward the sofa. "She's wrong about two things," the very, deep voice said.

His words echoed around the room. "Holy shit," Marci said and grabbed Mike's arm.

"I can speak. And you won't be rid of ghosts when you leave. Because everywhere you go, you'll see dead people. Remember this important thing. Some of us are nicer than others. I'm here with you because there is a serial killer ghost who followed you here. I'm trying to keep him away."

Marci sighed.

Great Johnny Appleseed didn't tell her that.

Janet screamed from the other room. She threw the bedroom door open. "There's another ghost in our room! He's not very nice."

# CORA FOERSTNER

Author of the Dragon Speakers Duology



# THE UNINTENDED HERO

A Spooky Short Story

5

# THE UNINTENDED HERO

Robert Ramsey awoke in an unknown location. His mind and everything about him went from being out of it in the dark to being awake in a world of green grass.

His body was stretched out on the grass, looking up. There were trees, tall ones . . . pine trees swaying in the wind. The smell of freshly mowed grass. Green he realized grass was the smell of color. He smiled amused. He had never thought of colors as having smells.

There was a breeze, but he couldn't feel it. He saw it as the trees swayed. An occasional raindrop fell on his face. The drop came down so slowly he could see it splatter on his face.

His first thought was . . . this is weird.

It was an odd, different, freaking experience. He watched the trees to see the wind. When he concentrated very, very hard on feeling the wind on his face, it moved across his body like a feather tickling his skin.

Another oddity.

He saw water pooled on the grass, but his clothes weren't wet. He wasn't cold. Maybe he was having a virtual experience, like someone using a virtual machine. He'd never used one, but he'd seen it on cable TV.

Also why couldn't he smell the grass? Or feel cold? Or hear birds? He chuckled. Birds were smart enough not to be in a puddle of water while it was raining.

Little pictures kept flashing in his mind. A crazy man, wild eyes, mouth twisted in a grin that made Robert feel queasy.

Robert was shouting, "Run! Run! Run! Keep running!"

Then someone was holding him, crying.

He realized that none of the images or words comforted him. The imaginings were from the dark place. Now, he was in the green place where he didn't get wet, even lying in a puddle. The wind and rain didn't make him cold.

Yeah, he was dreaming. This was a big, fat, excellent dream.

There was a girl . . . a pretty girl with long brown hair and a nice smile. She'd smiled at him, but she was also crying. Then his memories jumped around and jumbled together.

He remembered the doctors and nurses talking about him. His mother crying and the doctor sending her away. Then everything was quiet. All the talking and beeping and machine noises stopped.

Darkness surrounded him.

Now the world was green, cloudy, and real. He awoke on the ground, not in a bed. He sat on wet grass in drizzling rain. He looked down. He had a suit on. The one his father bought him for an interview.

He couldn't remember what interview. College? Yes, college. Then that memory floated away. Confusion replaced the memory. His mind moved from one thing to another. He couldn't put it all together.

Did the doctors throw him out of the hospital? Why? Maybe he was better? He remembered being hurt.

He had to call his parents. He searched his pockets for a phone. Nothing. His pockets were empty. He couldn't even find lint.

He stood and glanced around. Next to him was a grave marker, about a foot and a half high. He glanced left and found a row of grave markers. He looked right, more gravestones. These were flat and embedded in the ground.

In the distance, he saw fancy headstones, one had an angel with its wings spread over the ground, others were plain. There were crosses.

The grass was green. Yeah, he'd noticed that when he first woke up. His clothes weren't getting wet, but they should have been wet. The light rain continued to fall. The wind was blowing the trees.

He should be cold.

Why wasn't he cold? Why wasn't he wet?

He glanced down. Embedded in the short green grass was a marker. The engraving read:

Robert J. Ramsey 2007 - 2025
Beloved son and brother.
An angel sent to us for too short a time.

He sat on the narrow concrete path that separated one row of graves from another. Sitting cross-legged, he stared at the engraving. He squinted at the words.

His name and birth year.

He was dead.

Did he die in the hospital? Why?

He couldn't remember.

Had he been sick?

Oh, yeah, a crazy man . . . high on something . . . he was robbing the gas station store.

He glanced down the long concrete walkway or sidewalk. A girl about his age carried a bouquet of flowers, every color, red, purple, yellow, pink, white. She strolled along the path, reading the gravestones, and moving along slowly.

She had long brown hair. Brown eyes. Sad eyes. Someone she loved was here. She was bringing flowers. She looked kind.

No, he couldn't really tell if she was kind. She was pretty, so maybe that made her look kind.

When she came to one of the graves a few feet away from him, she stopped on the other side of the narrow sidewalk. She sobbed or maybe moaned. She sounded sad.

He guessed she'd found the gravestone she had been searching for . . . who was it?

He walked to the grave and stood beside her. She didn't notice him.

The main thing he felt was lonely.

He looked down at the epitaph.

Susan Jean Gordon
2021 - 2022
Beautiful and Loved.

Ah, a little sadness washed over him. That's why the girl was sad. The time of the Covid pandemic . . . poor little girl didn't ever get to grow up.

The pretty girl took one yellow rose from the bouquet she carried. Bending down, she placed the flower on the baby girl's gravestone.

He expected her to turn and leave, but she didn't. She walked right through him as if he didn't exist. She didn't pause or hesitate.

He followed her. "Miss, Miss, can I ask you a question?"

He tried to touch her shoulder, but his hand went right through her body. That's when he took a good look at his body. His body was there—hands, arms, torso, legs, feet, but he wasn't completely solid. Like his body was slowly turning to smoke.

Again, he followed her as she looked at gravestones. He spoke to her, but she continued to ignore him.

In that moment, he admitted to himself what he knew all along. He was a ghost. He hadn't wanted to admit it. Most of all, he didn't want to be a ghost.

He thought ghosts were supposed to be scary. He certainly didn't feel scary or mean or angry.

He spotted a bench in the distance. Hurrying forward he sat and looked around.

Was he stuck here?

Sitting on the bench was better than the grass. His mother wouldn't be happy if he got grass stains on his pants. He shrugged. He guessed that didn't matter anymore. Nothing mattered.

The girl turned around and walked back again reading the gravestones on the other side. She stopped in front of his small rectangular slab. She fell to her knees. Wet spots appeared where her legs touched the wet grass. Her jeans had spots on her knees. She didn't seem to care.

She pressed her lips together as if she were holding back tears. Robert recognized her. She was the girl at the gas station.

Robert remembered pumping gas. He could smell it on his hands as he opened the door to the gas station's little store. It looked like all the other gas station stores he'd been in. Small with rows and rows of junk food and sundry items. The two outside walls were lined with refrigerators. All he wanted was soda for his ride home.

He stopped and held the door open.

A man with wild eyes and blond hair pulled into a ponytail held a gun in his hand. That's all he could remember about the man . . . his wild eyes.

"Open the cash register! Now! Now!"

The clerk's hands were raised and shaking. He saw Robert standing there with the door open. The clerk slowly with an almost imperceptible movement shook his head as he moved toward the cash register.

Robert started to back up. He planned to go outside and call the police. Then he saw the girl. She had earphones on, moving gracefully and swaying to music. She opened the refrigerator door and grabbed a diet soda. She looked about his age, a beautiful teenage girl.

When she turned toward him and saw him in the door, he put his index finger to his lips. He pointed to the cash register. He waved his hand downward, hoping she'd know to get down and hide.

She immediately bent down and scooted to the side, behind the end of the shelf. She looked so scared. She put her hand over her mouth. Her brown eyes were round and frightened.

Robert could smell gas from the outside, coffee, and the spicy aroma of hot dogs turning on a spit.

The night air was cold, too cold to stand there with the door open.

He was afraid to move because the man might see him. What he hadn't counted on was the girl's movement. She tried to move further back. Her movement flashed in the round mirror attached to the wall above the clerk.

That mirror showed the girl, crouched down at the back of the aisle.

When the man turned and pointed the gun at her, she gasped. Her eyes looked at Robert. He hadn't moved.

Fear, the kind that made his stomach revolt and his hands shake, gripped his body. He couldn't move. The man stared at the girl. Any second, the man would notice him.

Robert saw terror in her eyes. Terror worse than the fear he felt. She was in the man's sight.

At that moment, it seemed as if the whole world had stopped. The clerk froze with his hand in the cash register and bills in one hand as his gaze went to the girl. His face grew even paler than it had been.

The girl held her hand over her mouth, still as a marble statue unable to move because her gaze was fixed on the man.

"Stand up!"

She didn't move.

"I said . . . stand UP!"

The clerk dropped the money and ducked behind the counter.

The gunman turned toward the clerk.

"Run! Run!" Robert waved her forward. "Run!"

He held the door open wider. She ran.

Robert stepped back to let her pass.

She ran through the open door.

"Run! Keep running!"

Robert let go of the door. He moved to follow the girl.

The gunman turned toward him, raising the hand-gun. Robert rolled to the ground, away from the door. He heard a shot.

His phone in his hand, he pressed 911. It hurt to breathe.

"Robber . . . gunshots. Main and . . . South Eighth. Gas station."

Robert lifted his head up in time to see the clerk hit the shooter with a baseball bat.

In the distance, a siren's wail . . . getting closer.

There was red on the front of his hoodie.

The clerk kicked the gun the robber dropped out of the away. The gunman was on the ground begging the clerk not to hurt him.

Robert couldn't stand up. He tried. Then he tried again. It was easier to stay still.

Then the girl was there. Holding him. Crying.

He wasn't sure why she was crying. The bullet must have hit her. There was blood on her hands.

He tried to move to help her.

Those were images that his mind put in the right order.

In the cemetery, he watched the girl reach over and rub her hand over the engraving on his gravestone. Then she put the rest of the flowers on the ground.

"I wish you could hear me," she said. "Thank you. You saved my life. I went to your funeral. I stayed in the back, so your parents didn't see me. I thought they might feel sad seeing the girl who lived. Thank you."

She kissed her fingers and touched his name again.

He moved closer to her and put his hand on her shoulder. This time his hand stayed there. It didn't go through her body.

"I hear you," he whispered.

Out of nowhere, a woman appeared close to the girl. She sat next to the girl.

"Hello, my name is Ginny," she said.

The girl looked surprised for a moment. "Hi, I'm Zoe."

"He's here," Ginny looked at his name. "Robert. He's a ghost. I see ghosts. He's handsome in a teenage kind of way. When you spoke, he put his hand on your shoulder and said 'I hear you.'"

"You're freaking me out, Ginny."

"Yeah, people say that a lot."

Robert glanced around. No one else was around.

"Tell her I'm okay. Well, I think I'm okay. I'm sort of a ghost. I don't know what that means."

Ginny repeated his words.

"Are you just playing some sort of a prank on me?" Zoe asked.

"No, you seemed sad, so I thought I'd tell you what he said. He's a new ghost so he doesn't know what he's doing yet. He's making things up as he goes. He'll learn to communicate."

"Is his hand still on my shoulder?"

Ginny nodded and pointed to Zoe's right shoulder.

Zoe grew very still. She slowly reached her hand up, and laid her hand over his.

"Tell her I'm happy she's alive."

Ginny frowned at him and shook her head.

"Then tell her something nice."

"He said that you should live life to the fullest and be happy. Don't worry about him. He'll probably go to the light soon."

Zoe leaned over and kissed Ginny on the cheek. "Give him that kiss for me."

"He saw you kiss my cheek and smiled. Is that good enough?"

"It is," Zoe said, as she stood up and dusted off her jeans. "Thank you, Robert and Ginny. I'll come back." She walked toward the street and turned back. "Teach him how you made yourself seem real. Then he can talk to me, right?"

"Right," Ginny said.

Robert watched Zoe walk away. She glanced back and waved. If he were alive, he might have a crush on a pretty girl.

"You look silly," Ginny said. "It's a good thing she can't see you. She'd laugh at your big cow eyes and silly smile."

He squinted at Ginny. There was something a little off about her. He couldn't put his finger on it. Then in a flash of insight, he knew.

Long straight blond hair. A multi-colored headband. Big, big-ass bell bottoms, and sandals suitable for summer, not a cold rainy fall day. She was a ghost too.

He pointed to her and smiled.

She looked up and sighed. "It took you long enough. Zoe figured it out right away. What did she thank you for?"

"I saved her life." He heard the pride in his voice and felt a little embarrassed.

"And you died in the process . . . not smart in the living world. You should take better care of yourself."

"The man who was going to shoot her, shot me."

"So you're a dumbass. I can teach you to take on corporeal form. If she comes back, it might come in handy."

"She won't come back, but I wouldn't mind knowing how to take on corporeal form. I'm not entirely sure what corporeal means."

"It means a body . . . like a real person. I look real and am solid."

"Yes, I want to learn that. Who taught you?"

"Reggie. You'll meet him soon. He might even let you haunt his big old mansion. He's a ghost too. His daughter runs an inn in Bluefield. She's alive. It's kind of fun to go to the inn. In the summer, there's a pool to swim in."

"I've heard of the place. I thought it was a joke. You do know ghosts aren't real."

"I heard that rumor." She nodded her head toward the back of the cemetery. "Come on. I'll introduce you to the others."

As they walked, she sang some old song that was probably from the 1970s. She had a pretty good voice. Maybe he'd teach her some modern songs.

"So, you'll really teach me how to be corporeal and then I can talk to her?"

"Sure I can, but you said she wasn't coming back."

He grinned. He knew it was a lopsided grin because everyone said he had a cute lopsided grin. "Maybe she will come back."

Ginny put her arm around his shoulder. "I kinda like you, kid. One warning . . . ghosts can't fall in love with the living. Well, I guess they can, but it's a one-sided thing."

It was too late for that warning. Besides, he'd already figured that out.

# CORA FOERSTNER

Author of the Dragon Speakers Duology

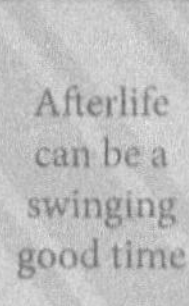



# Finding Redemption

A Spooky Short Story

6

---

# FINDING REDEMPTION

## 1. CYNTHIA: GOING TOO FAST

Cynthia stared out the passenger window, watching the scenery fly past. Reggie drove too fast. If she watched the road, anxiety took over.

She'd already asked him to slow down, which he did for about two minutes. Without looking at him, she knew he was relaxed, driving with one hand on the wheel. His steel blue eyes, partly glancing at the road and partly watching the passing scenery. He listened to some know-it-all guru talking about business.

She focused on spring in Washington state.

Warmer weather and rain always brought a riot of growth. The deciduous trees still had new leaves. The yellowish greens that would soon be darker and greener. All the different kinds of pine trees stood out among the new leaves. With their varieties of dark greens, they looked older, more mature compared to the shiny yellow-green leaves of the deciduous trees.

A house with yellow daffodils and every shade of tulips imaginable flew by a flash of color. She smiled. She imagined some woman with small children had planted the flowers. She wished she'd been that kind of mother, barefoot and playing in the grass with her children, cutting the spring flowers to take inside.

Their new navy blue Cadillac Lyriq drove like a dream, smooth and comfortable. If she closed her eyes, she'd think they were barely moving. She couldn't complain. Well, except for the fact she thought the car was ugly and embarrassingly pretentious.

The black grill on the front and the lights shaped like a triangle pointing toward the grill reminded her of a badly drawn animated car. It might look fine for a children's movie.

Speed was another matter. Yes, the car could go fast if that was something a person wanted. Reggie drove as if the devil were chasing him. He always drove too fast. She had always hated it.

"Someday, you're going to get us killed." She couldn't count the times she'd said that.

In the old days, they drove a clunker and sang along to the playlists Reggie made back then. When they got tired of singing, they'd talk about their dreams and hopes. She'd laughed because they were young and happy.

Back then Reggie smiled all the time. He took her dancing, and made up silly songs to entertain her. The memories made her sigh.

She glanced upward. The azure sky had changed to gray as clouds gathered overhead and blocked out the sun. Instead of afternoon, it looked like twilight.

The phone rang. Reggie answered from a button on the steering wheel. A button she pretended she didn't know how to use.

The car politely turned off the music. David, one of Reggie's managers, spoke softly in a kind, gentle voice. She braced herself. She glanced at her watch. It took Reggie one and a half minutes before he started yelling.

If she were in charge of the world, she'd make it illegal to have phone conversations while driving. Think of how much better David would feel if the owner of the company weren't yelling at him. Think of how much better she'd feel if Reggie's foot hadn't pushed the gas pedal harder.

Sometimes she wondered if a person's heart could explode from irritability. She decided to ignore the yelling and concentrate on the beauty around her.

They were heading home to Bluefield. A tiny town tucked in the forest between Seattle and Woodinville. Scenic, that is what everyone called Bluefield. Only she knew the small town was dying, a slow, slow death. The man sitting next to her was responsible for its future demise.

Although Reggie continued to berate him, David kept a pleasant almost soothing voice. The contrast was striking. That voice did nothing to calm Reggie.

Apparently, David was too soft. Didn't have his people in control.

"So what if some woman's child was sick. Tell her to hire a babysitter."

She glared at Reggie. She thought about reminding him that he didn't pay his employees enough money to hire a sitter. Instead, she looked at the sky again.

Rain from heaven, um that sounded like a song. At first it was a few drops on the windshield. Then it got a little more forceful. The wipers came on. The swish, slap sound softened Reggie's voice. Strange that she couldn't even hear rain pelting the car.

She loved the rain. But not driving in it at top speed. Home in front of the fire, reading a book and watching the rain drops hitting the bedroom balcony, that was her idea of a lovely afternoon.

Keller's factory and stores brought in millions. Probably billions. Especially during and after the pandemic, when everyone learned to shop online.

She didn't know their worth because apparently she was a fragile flower. Numbers and dollar signs might explode her brain. What Reggie didn't know was she had over three million dollars she'd saved from her obscene allowance.

Yeah, they were rich. Their employees weren't. Bunny, their golden retriever, had a better dog house than some of their employees' houses.

Those facts like cancer ate at her soul.

She glanced at her husband. His flushed face looked cartoonish as if smoke would shoot out of his ears at any moment. She thought about telling him he was going too fast but reconsidered.

Reggie went off on another rant as David listened and every once in a while made a noise that sounded like he at least heard what Reggie had said.

Cynthia read the subtext to mean, *You're a nasty old man. I hate my job. I hate the company. Most of all I hate you. I'm stuck here with you and can't afford to leave.*

She knew exactly how he felt. Of course, she really couldn't point a finger because she'd realized too late that she'd turned into a nasty, mean old woman, who hated her life, and most of all hated the woman she'd become.

At fifty-eight, she saw her reflection in the window and realized she didn't like herself. It wasn't her slightly sagging jawline or the wrinkles around her eyes. It was her insides that were rotting.

She wanted to fill her front yard with daffodils and tulips, to dance in the rain, and to laugh as she had when she was young. She wanted to sing with the man she'd married so many years ago and laugh at his silly jokes.

In many ways, she and Reggie deserved each other. She'd been trying for two weeks to tell him she wanted to leave. They couldn't divorce because as Reggie had told her when he asked her to marry him, divorce is too expensive. So, marriage is forever.

Of course that was true, but she could live in their vacation home on Whedbey Island. She could make friends, go for walks, and maybe do something meaningful, something helpful.

One of those huge delivery trucks honked as it drove past them. Dirty water from the truck splattered their windshield. She glanced at the speedometer. They were going eighty. The trucker was going faster.

The car shook. Fear shot through her body like a warning.

Reggie swerved and shouted a string of colorful metaphors that would cause a sailor to blush. It was her understanding that sailors used profane language that caused people to blush. She'd never known any sailors, but she assumed profanity ran wild among sailors.

That was when she noticed something strange. Indeed, it was extremely strange and curiously interesting. Their big ugly Cadillac was spinning across the highway. In slow motion, each turn lasting and lasting and lasting.

The funniest thing was her brain was telling her that the car had to be spinning very fast. It wasn't. They were turning slowly, like when a streaming movie goes slow because the connection isn't good. Of course that was wrong because movies didn't do that any more.

As they turned, their lights illuminated the car behind them. A blond man in the passenger seat shielded his eyes from their headlights. He pointed at them and shouted something to the man driving.

For some reason the car wasn't getting closer to them. She expected the SUV to plow into them, but as their car turned, the other car was still behind them. She saw the whole thing in milliseconds like individual frames of a film slowly moving past them.

As they turned, Reggie glanced at her with his steel blue eyes wide like a child who skinned his knee and held back tears. His mouth opened as if to speak. She didn't hear any words.

His hand reached for her.

She smiled, happy at that moment. That was the nicest thing he'd done in years. The Cadillac managed to cross the highway without anyone hitting the car behind them.

She held out her hand and took his.

The car didn't stop. It flew off the road right where the road curved.

She knew there was a pretty good drop. How deep of a drop she didn't know. The car hovered in the air for what seemed like a long time before it dropped. It hit the side of the cliff.

Then bounced, one, twice, three times. The car

turned like a child's toy. Her seat belt pulled her tight.

She told herself that the airbags would keep them safe. Reggie held her hand. The headlights illuminated the steep fall just as the car slammed into a huge old pine tree.

The tree had probably been growing for a hundred years or more. The words, *sorry old boy*, crossed her mind. Her next thought was she couldn't really call a tree old boy. But she had.

For a long second everything went silent and peaceful. The airbags released, a little late she thought as the bag slammed into her body, breaking her nose for sure. She'd complain about that to Cadillac.

Her face hurt like hell. She still held Reggie's hand. Everything went black.

## 2. REGGIE: HALLUCINATIONS

Reggie had blacked out. He remembered his body hurting, especially his face. Now, he didn't feel any pain. He touched his face, there were no cuts, nothing felt bruised.

My luck is holding out, he told himself. Too bad about the car. Insurance will handle it.

He reached for the door handle. His hand seemed to go right through it. Yet, he stepped through a solid door and got out of the car. He hurried around the back to reach Cynthia. Again his hand went through the door. He'd think about that later.

PTSD?

Hallucinations? Maybe?

He chuckled. David. He'd been talking to him. He'd heard the crash. He'd probably called the police. They'd be here soon.

He grabbed Cynthia's arm and pulled her out of the car. That was strange too. Her body slid right through the seatbelt and the door.

Yeah, hallucination. They'd laugh about his wild imagination later.

Right now, they stood on a wide ridge. Cynthia walked to the edge and glanced down. He followed her. If it hadn't been for the tree, they would have fallen another twenty or more feet.

Good thing they hit the tree.

"How are you?" Reggie asked as he patted himself down. "I seem to be fine. No cuts or bruises."

Cynthia opened her mouth to speak, but her gaze turned toward the car. She pointed.

Reggie glanced at the car. The airbags had deployed. It looked like he was still in the car. Cynthia sat in the passenger seat. The side of her face smashed against the airbag.

She was smiling at him. He was looking at her. She looked so happy. He hadn't seen her happy in a long time. Well, whatever she was smiling about, it sure wasn't the accident.

He stepped closer to the car. Of course, he was having some sort of post-traumatic response to the accident. One of his employees told him that once. He dismissed it as an excuse for being a snowflake. Eventually he fired the guy.

Maybe he'd been wrong? The man had called it a near death experience. Maybe he hadn't made up an excuse? Maybe it was real. That was a hell of a lot of maybes.

"Reggie, why are we still in the car, not moving?"

Standing beside her he glanced into the car, squinting. He had a similar response to what he saw.

"I think we are dead," she said.

"No, we aren't dead. I feel fine."

"That means nothing. Neither of us has been dead before. There's no way to know how it feels."

She glanced up. Two men stood on the side of the road staring down at them. They must have seen the accident.

Cynthia waved. "We need some help."

Neither man responded.

"They can't hear us," Reggie said. "The rain and the traffic blunt the sound of our voices."

"We're dead. I'm sure of it." She stepped to the edge of the ledge. "Do you think we have to spend the rest of eternity here? It'll be rather cold in the winter."

"I'm going to climb up," Reggie said. "We aren't dead."

She stood there and watched him climb. That was her way, let him do whatever he wanted. If she really thought they were dead, she should have tried to convince him.

He climbed a few feet. Grabbed a tree root that jetted out of the dirt. His hand slid through the root. He slid downward. He tried six or seven times.

Sanding back, he analyzed the problem. Between rocks, bushes, and roots, there were plenty of solid places to hold on and climb. But he couldn't hold on. It was like there was something wrong with his hands. He didn't really have a grip. He'd have to get that checked out.

He gave up. They'd have to wait for the police to arrive. The police would have something to bring them up.

Reggie glanced at Cynthia. She looked a little weird like an old black and white photo that had faded, making it hard to see the people in the picture.

"Cynthia, you're fading."

"What do you mean by fading?"

"You're getting lighter and lighter. I can almost see through you."

She looked down. "You're right I can barely see my body. It's translucent."

She frowned and pointed to him. So he looked at himself.

His clothes, his arms, legs, feet were nearly gone. Translucent. She was right.

"Do you believe me now? We are ghosts. Dead ghosts."

Reggie sat on a large boulder. Green moss covered it. He knew she'd think that insects and other things were inside the moss. He motioned her to sit on the smaller boulder.

She found a flat thin stone and used it to scrape some of the moss off her boulder. She didn't seem to have trouble picking things up. He couldn't hold onto anything.

He grinned as he watched her. She didn't find anything creepy crawlies in the moss, so she sat.

"Why are you ginning?" she asked.

"You're cute." He shrugged.

"We are ghosts. I wouldn't call that cute."

The unsettling thought that they might vanish and not be able to see each other frightened him.

"You know I think we are supposed to see a light and go toward it," she said.

"All I see is rain," he said, trying to lighten things up a bit.

It didn't take much imagination to know that she was right. Two bodies in the car. No cuts, or bruises or anything from the crash on them. Most of all they were definitely fading away.

For the first time in years, Reggie sat quietly thinking. He wasn't sure how much time passed. The phone was in the car. He didn't want to go poking around their dead bodies. So, he waited.

What was he waiting for? He didn't know.

Finally, very fit firefighters repelled down the cliff. He and Cynthia hadn't completely vanished, but the firefighters didn't see them. The female walked around the car and glanced inside.

"They're dead," she called out. "Probably the impact of hitting the tree. They're kinda cute. They are holding hands and smiling at each other."

"See," Cynthia said.

"Lisa, you are the most sentimental person I know." The older man with the bluest eyes he'd ever seen walked around and glanced in the car.

"She's right," the third firefighter said. "They are sorta cute. Too bad they're dead."

Reggie could see the man was fit and healthy, and probably about his age. He wished he'd gone to the gym more. Looking at the front of the car all caved him, he knew being fit wouldn't have saved him.

The firefighters worked in the rain. They had to cut through the windows to open the doors and get them out.

"They're very respectful," Cynthia said.

Her voice sounded surprised. Reggie had been quiet the entire time. He had a lot of thinking to do. Like how were they going to get up that cliff. He certainly didn't want to stay here haunting a cliff.

And where was the white light everyone talked about? Pretty hard to go toward a light if you can see it. Maybe he should have a look around.

By the time the firefighters hauled the gurneys

with their bodies up, tow trucks arrived to pull the car up.

"This isn't going to work," Reggie finally said. "We can't sit here on this ledge for eternity. We could, but it would be awfully boring and tedious."

Behind them someone cleared his throat. Cynthia screamed and jumped up, looking behind her. Reggie stood and pulled Cynthia behind him.

A very tall man, with blondish hair that was a little too long, smiled at them. He dressed in a black turtleneck sweater, black pants, and looked exactly like Alan Rickman, who was also dead.

Wouldn't that make a good story at the club? We died and Alan Rickman came to take us to the light.

"I beg your pardon. I didn't mean to frighten you."

Cynthia stepped out from behind Reggie. "Alan? Rickman? Have you come to take us to the light."

"No. And no. My name is Raymond, protector of men and women. Cynthia, moon goddess, an interesting name. Reginald, ruler's advisor, doesn't quite fit, does it. You're the ruler not the advisor."

"Oh," Cynthia said and scooted back behind Reggie.

Reggie didn't know one thing about ghosts. He did know that this ghost spoke oddly. The name's thing was pretty weird. Maybe the fellow was senile? He didn't seem dangerous, but Cynthia was wise to be cautious.

"Going to the light is a human myth. I've come with some good news and some bad news."

"It doesn't take a genius to fetter out the bad news. We are dead." Reggie folded his arms over his chest and started at Raymond.

"Well yes, there is that, but that's not the entirety of the bad news."

"Oh, you've come to escort us to heaven." Cynthia said. "That's comforting. Reggie was just saying that spending eternity on this ledge would be unpleasant."

"Um, no heaven is another human myth that doesn't apply to me."

"You keep saying human myths. Why? Who are you?" Reggie continued with his arms folded and purposefully glared at Raymond.

"I am not human. I'm a guardian. I watch over this dimension. I take on human form because it makes people more accepting."

"That makes no sense and doesn't explain anything," Cynthia said.

"Yes, you are correct. So allow me to explain."

Reggie got the feeling this was this man's way of

saying shut up and let me talk. He could live with that. The man might be delusional, but he knew things they didn't.

"For the bad news first—"

"What could possibly be worse news than being dead?" Reggie asked.

"Dear, Raymond would like to explain. Save your questions."

Raymond nodded. Reggie unfolded his arms and sat on his boulder. Cynthia stood. It was still raining, but he wasn't cold. That was good news.

"The bad news is that you were not supposed to die today. The driver of the truck has a son. The boy was in an accident. He'll lose his leg today. He was rushing to the hospital unaware that he caused an accident. So, Reggie, you'll be stuck here for another eight years and Cynthia for longer. Until the appointed time, I was to move you along to another dimension. I may be able to change your timeline. We'll see."

"Then we go to heaven?" Cynthia said.

Raymond shook his head. "Unfortunately unless you undo the damage you've done, you'll be going to an unpleasant dimension."

"Hell, just say it man," Reggie said. "What have we done that's so bad to deserve hell?"

Raymond pulled out a thick folder and a book, handing them to Cynthia.

"The book explains everything about your state of being. The folder is an account of your life. You have eight years to correct your deeds. If you can do that, then things will be much better for you."

"Good deeds. I've seen the movie. How do we do a good deed if our bodies are fading. We need ectoplasm."

Raymond's eyebrows shot up and formed a pyramid that wrinkled his forehead.

"I'm unfamiliar with ectoplasm, but the book explains how to conserve your energy so your body will take a corporeal form."

"Ectoplasm does that. It gives your body mass, so people can hear and see you."

"How do we get off this ledge?" Cynthia asked.

"If we have corporeal bodies can we drive, eat, talk to people," Reggie asked.

"In time, certainly. I'll make a portal to your home. Read the book and study it. Also," Raymond took two small phones from his pocket and tossed one to Reggie and one to Cynthia, who dropped it into the mud. She picked it up and wiped it on her pant leg. "It's a computer. You can ask Bella for help. She can explain things."

They followed Raymond into a shimmering opening. Cynthia went first. Reggie hesitated a moment, wondering why they were listening to this guy. Finally he stepped in and discovered they were in the entryway of their home. When he turned to talk to Raymond, the man wasn't there.

"I'm going to think of him as our guardian angel. He said he was a protector of men and women," Cynthia said.

Although he didn't like the man because his social behavior seemed strange, Reggie agreed with his wife. Angel sounded better than Guardian, which sounded suspiciously like a prison guard.

She hurried up the split staircase to their bedroom. Reggie followed her. She sat on the bed reading the book. She glanced up.

"I found the ectoplasm part," Cynthia said and read a long boring paragraph.

"So we stay faded to conserve ectoplasm, but the book calls it energy. I could go through and change the words to ectoplasm."

A hologram of a young girl with purple pigtails and a dress that reminded Reggie of a Cinderella dress from one of his daughter's old storybooks.

Cynthia squealed. "Who are you?"

"Bella. I will change the book to read ectoplasm. Also anything else you need, simply call my name."

"Ookaay," Cynthia said.

"Who are you? How did you just appear? Why are you wearing that silly dress?"

"Reggie, don't disparage her dress. Maybe she's going to a fancy party."

Reggie shook his head and rolled his eyes.

"I'm Bella. I'm a computer program. I'm a lot more advanced than current technology. I can help you with this transition. I'm a hologram. I like this dress. I saw it in an old book your daughter treasured. I thought the dress might be familiar and calm you."

Reggie stared at her. For the first time since the accident, he wondered if he were imagining all this. Maybe he was in the hospital in a coma? Maybe this was a dream?

"All right," Reggie said. "Ectoplasm makes us solid. We can talk to people, people can see us, and we can touch things and do things."

"Yes, that's a good description of *energyum*. Call my name if you need anything. Just say Bella and I will appear."

Reggie stared at Cynthia who seemed unfazed by

some strange hologram talking to them. She was reading the damn book.

"It says here," Cynthia said. "We can see each other when we are faded, but regular people can't see us. There are some people who do see dead people. So don't be surprised if some people do see us. Often a child can see ghosts. Don't you think that might disturb a child?"

Reggie noticed that there was a kindness about Cynthia that he remembered from when they were younger.

"I think that would depend on the child," he said. "You know how some kids have imaginary friends? Maybe they are just seeing ghosts."

Cynthia looked up at Reggie. "You might be right. In that case they wouldn't be frightened of the ghost."

"Well, unless the ghost is evil."

Cynthia squinted at Reggie. "Must you always go to a dark place? Go take a shower and change. You're muddy."

She went to her little Japanese desk and took out paper and pen.

"What are you doing?"

"I'll tell you when you get back. You can move things by thinking your hand is solid. That's the ectoplasm at work. You can use it up, so use it sparingly."

She was a bossy ghost. When he went into the bathroom, he could see himself in the mirror. He looked normal.

Thinking about his hand being solid was far more difficult than it sounded. He failed in the thinking solid department. Did ghosts really need to shower? He glanced at his shoes and pants. Mud cover his shoe and the hem of his trousers.

More important than showering was figuring out what they had done wrong. How did you fix something if you didn't know the problem? Raymond said they had to fix things. What things? That would have been a good question to ask the very strange man.

Reggie had done everything right. He'd never killed anyone, or physically harmed anyone, or cheated on his taxes. Well, he'd cheated a little once, but the guilt made him miserable. He'd made billions, supported his family, and gave his kids a good education.

All things considered, he didn't think it would be difficult to fix things and move on to a better place. He was going to think of it as heaven, even if Raymond dismissed the idea.

Of course, he started remembering things that

he'd done that had bothered him. Cut corners. Fired people who were desperate. Cheated on safety measures.

Maybe these things were the problem. In that case, this wasn't going to be as easy as he thought.

On the other hand, he knew people who'd done far worse things. He wondered if that counted. He was not as bad as old George.

## 3. ERIC: BAD NEWS

Eric, Reggie and Cynthia's youngest son, woke early. He grabbed some coffee, and left Portland, Oregon headed for Bluefield, Washington. Dawn still had that hazy limbo look of almost light but not quite. The sun barely painted yellows and oranges across the sky as Eric pulled onto the I5 freeway heading north. The traffic was light. Even before the morning rush hour started, he'd crossed the state line, and drove past Vancouver and exited I5 to head toward the coast.

The first part of his journey, he followed the Pacific Coast shoreline to enjoy the view of the

Puget Sounds. He loved seeing the bridges that went from the mainland over to the small islands. The evergreens, the deciduous trees with their new pale green leaves, meadows, the wild flowers, and ocean views relaxed him.

It was the long way to Bluefield. The freeway was faster, but Eric felt the need to experience the sights of nature. Seeing the ocean, sleepy communities, and distant islands somehow reminded him that life was more than work and business.

He planned to arrive at his parents house early, so he could tell his father and mother that he was resigning from the board. He wanted to do something different. Help people, not make more and more money.

His mother would hug him and give her blessing. His father would blow up, or storm off, or pressure him into reconsidering.

Eric worried that he would give in to the pressure.

He wasn't exactly dissatisfied with his life, but he longed for something more. He just didn't know what that was.

Once he got closer to Seattle, he headed back to I5 where he couldn't see much expect for freeways, cars, and trucks. He'd checked the weather report before leaving. He knew heavy rainfall around the Seattle area was expected in the morning forecast. He would hit some of it before reaching his parents' home.

He was a cautious driver so bad weather didn't bother him. His father drove like a wild man. A shrink would tell him that his cautious driving was simply over compensating for his father's reckless driving. He was happy to over compensate.

If the rain got bad, he'd stop and wait. He'd grown up in Washington and spring storms often dissipated quickly. On the other hand, sometimes they lasted all day.

Eric turn the radio on to wash away those thoughts. He didn't need to think about a confrontation with his parents.

He wanted to dedicate more time and energy to Lawyers Without Borders. Somehow his mother always seemed to understand him. She'd probably hug him and whisper that he should do what he wanted, but she'd never tell his father that. Well, it was what it was.

He'd just turned off the I5 on to the 405 going toward Renton, when his phone rang. He let it go to voice mail so the car's computer could read the message. His sister Hannah's voice message, played.

*Eric, I'll call back in five minutes, pick up. Don't mess around with me. I have tragic news.*

He doubted the news was tragic in the sense that most people thought of tragedy. Hannah's last melodramatic news was that her favorite soap opera star died of an overdose.

He'd answer her next call and consoled her.

Exactly five minutes later, his phone rang again. He pressed the answer phone button on his steering wheel'

He called out, "Hello, Hannah."

All he heard on the other end were sobs, real gut punching weeping. He felt a little guilty about dismissing her message.

"Hannah, take a deep breath and let it out slowly."

He heard her breathe and a slow exhale. She breathed again and again. The she began weeping again.

"Hannah. Hannah," his brother Owen said in the background.

Eric heard the phone making a scratching noise. Maybe she dropped it. There were whispers in the background. Then Owen's voice boomed into his car.

"Eric, it's Owen. Hannah can't talk. She wanted to tell you herself, but that's not going to work."

He heard Hannah whispering in the background.

"Owen, what's going on?"

"Crap, Eric, there's no easy way to say this."

There was a long pause of nothing but Owen's breathing.

Eric wasn't sure if he should be annoyed by their antics or if there was something wrong.

"There's been an accident," Owen whispered. "Mom and dad's car went over a cliff and hit a tree."

The words hit him like a giant fist slamming into his chest. For a second or two, he couldn't breathe as he waited for Owen to finish, but only silence surrounded him.

He took a deep breath and exhale slowly. An invisible hand squeezed his heart.

"How bad are they?"

More silence. Eric's heart pounded in his chest, his neck, his heart. The thumps continues as the only sound he could hear was Owen's breathing and Hannah's sobs in the background.

"Owen, how bad?"

"They . . . um, . . ."

Eric gripped the stirring wheel as his throat constricted.

"Um, . . . the paramedics said it was instantaneous. They both died instantly."

He let silent seconds tic by. His chest ached so bad he wondered if he were having a heart attack. No, of course, he wasn't.

"Eric?"

"Yeah, yeah. I'm here. I'm just shocked. Like I can't believe . . . I don't have words."

"Sure. Sure. It still feels that way for us too. Can you come?"

"Actually, I'm on my way. We were supposed to have a board meeting. I'm just outside Renton. I only brought clothes for two days."

That was a stupid thing to say. He didn't know why he said it. How could he think about clothes right now.

"Sorry. I'm not thinking straight."

"Yeah, man, I get it. Um you should stay here at the house with Hannah." Then he whispered. "She's a mess."

"I'll be there as soon as I can. I'll drive straight through."

"Be careful, please." Owen's voice sounded desperate. "Drive carefully."

"Yeah, always. See you in a couple hours."

Reality hit Eric like a bolt of lightning. He'd been wrapped up in his own problems, making his world seem like everything. Then in a couple seconds his problems seemed trivial.

Owen was trying to keep it together. He knew Hannah couldn't. She had a tender heart. Owen had to be desperate. He hated to see Hannah upset.

For an instant his foot pressed down on the gas pedal and he zoomed past three cars before he realized what he was doing. He slowed.

He didn't realize he was crying until he tasted tears on his lips. He wipe his face and kept driving. When he stopped for gas, he went to the bathroom. He washed his hands with icy cold water, hoping the cold would ground him from the disconnect he felt.

The image he saw in the mirror looked like a stranger. The whites of his eyes were red, even his blue eyes look darker. He looked pale and sickly.

No wonder the gas station attended looked at him strangely. He definitely wasn't fit to be seen in public. When he got back in the car, he opened an off brand high caffeine drink and downed it as quickly as he could manage.

He'd practically lived on the stuff when he was in law school. It would keep him awake. He phoned his landlady while he drove and told her he didn't know when he'd be back and to gather his mail for him. She was a sweetheart. When she asked what was wrong, he couldn't bring himself to say the words, so he lied.

"Nothing. Just tired."

"Honey, I know better than that. When you feel like talking, you can tell me."

He turned on radio and found a rock station playing something he didn't recognize or care about. He turned up the sound and let the beat pulse through his body. Listening like a teenager trying to drowned out life, he let the music keep him sane.

He didn't know the words. Of course he didn't need the words. He needed something to keep his mind from strangling him.

When he got to his parents house, he needed to be in a state of mind to deal with whatever her found. At least Owen was with Hannah. She was their father's favorite. He regretted all the times he'd called her pampered. Sometimes he could be a jerk.

They would get through this. The worst news had already dropped. Nothing could be worse. At least he hoped nothing could be worse.

# 4. CYNTHIA: RIGHTING WRONGS

. . .

Cynthia sat in her bedroom reading and rereading the instructions on how to make their bodies solid. She could hear Reggie in their bathroom mumbling to himself. Finally, he called for help.

She found him standing inside the all glass shower, which was large enough for five or six people to shower at once. He stood with his hands on his hips. He couldn't turn on the shower. This ghost thing was definitely going to take some getting used to.

She and Reggie stood in the bathroom and practiced until Reggie managed to turn on the shower. According to the instructions, this was a woo-woo process of the mind, and a ghost willing his body to become solid. For some unknown reason, she learned faster than Reggie. This inability to catch on caused him to mumble a long string of curse words that became more colorful as he became more frustrated and angry.

Then he stopped and asked if cursing would count against his redemption. His seriousness sent Cynthia into uproarious laughter, which turned out to be contagious. After several minutes of unstoppable laughter, he tapped into his ectoplasm and turned on the water.

Cynthia hurried back to the bedroom. She sat at the black lacquered desk and took out their business stationary. She chose her fancy Namiki Yukari Maki-e Fountain pen Hannah gave her for Christmas. She loved the cherry blooms painted and lacquered into the body.

She loved Japanese art. One of her dreams had been to visit Japan. Her bedroom furnishings reflected that love. She sighed. That trip was out of the question now.

She picked up the pen and stared at the huge red fan on the wall above her dresser. She had to manage this in such a way that they could start making positive changes. The strange man said they had four years to do good deeds.

In black ink, she wrote in her neat, tidy handwriting. In the background she heard Reggie singing in the shower. He always did that. He couldn't sing very well. His voice was crap, but he loved singing. When they were young, he sang all the time. Now, he only sings the shower.

She hadn't noticed that in a long time.

Something in her mind clicked, and she knew exactly what she should do. Scribbling yesterday's date at the top of the page, she wrote frantically, stopping every once in a while to rest her hand.

Funny that it seemed to be cramping. After all she was dead. How could she feel a cramp?

She didn't have time to ponder. All she knew is that according to the man they talked to . . . Raymond, yeah, that was his name. They had to be better people, make things right. Reggie wasn't going to like it, but she'd put her foot down.

The shower stopped. She heard the water going down the drain. Strange. Reggie kept singing. She glanced at the half closed door. Maybe he was shaving. Did ghosts shave? She didn't know. They had a lot to learn.

She glanced around and sighed. This room was huge. She'd never paid much attention. Something about it seemed obscene, too much. That red and black bedspread cost five thousand dollars, or was it eight? She couldn't remember. That definitely fell into the obscene category.

She'd never stood up to Reggie, just went along with everything. Religious people called that something. She couldn't think of what it was, but she knew it wasn't good. Sort of like the people who stand by when someone's being mugged, or beaten, or raped. Not doing anything.

She'd been standing by for years.

Holy cow, she was complicit. That wasn't the religious word, but it was the correct word.

She took up the pen and wrote some more. When Reggie came out of the shower she pointed to the clothes she'd laid out for him. He dutifully started dressing.

"It's a little weird that I can shower and dress. I thought ghosts just went around looking horrible and scaring people."

"Don't be silly. We never believed in ghosts. How could we possibly know what they could or couldn't do."

"You're right," he said as he put one leg into his briefs. "I could go commando style. I could be a naked ghost."

Cynthia laughed. "Just get dressed. We have work to do."

He whistled as he dressed and glanced at her, frowning like he knew she was doing something he would hate. But he didn't say anything.

She glanced at him and watched him fade. He grinned and pointed to the door, which he walked through without a word.

She stopped and listed everything she knew they needed to do. Then she remembered Zoe . . . Zoe Henderson. Reggie would bulk, but Zoe was perfect.

How could they fix thirty years of bad in four short years? She was going to try if she had to take Reggie kicking and screaming with her.

Five pages later, she used a ruler to draw a line. Then she printed her name under it. She did the same for Reggie and three witnesses. She glanced at the first page. She'd put yesterday's date. On page five, she put yesterday's date next to all the names.

Then she let the ectoplasm fade away. She chuckled to herself. She remembered where Reggie got that word ectoplasm. An old black and white movie he loved when they were young, Cary Grant starred in the movie. He and his wife were ghosts. She couldn't remember the actress.

She wondered what happened to make her and Reggie change so much? It just happened slowly. Maybe they just forgot how much people struggled in this world. They certainly forgot how they struggled.

She paced the room for a moment. Then she decided to try walking through doors. What surprised her most was that walking through a door was easy-breezy.

Then she tried a wall, which was weird. She went right through the studs and the electrical. That made her wonder about electricity. Could she feel it if there was a short or something.

She popped in and out of all the rooms upstairs. Finally she went back to her room to see if Reggie was back. He wasn't. So she sat down and added things to the list she'd started. Then she ordered the list from most important to least.

"Well," she said aloud, "Eric's not going to like this."

Reggie picked that moment to return. He was chuckling.

"I've been everywhere. No one noticed me. Well, not true. Marta might have. She glanced at me and squinted. You know she believes in ghosts and stuff. *Bruja.* Yeah, she said her family had *brujas. Brujas blancas.*"

"That means white witches."

"I know. I remember some Spanish." Reggie shook his head. "That was a long time ago."

He plopped on the bed and sank through. He crawled out from under the bed.

"What happened?"

"According to the book Raymond gave us, you have to make a conscious determination not to fall through the things. Like standing on this floor, we expect to not fall through so we don't."

"How in the hell do you do that?"

"I think it's about the same as making your body solid. Try imagining sitting on the bed."

He fell through again. She laughed and moved to the bed and sat.

"How did you do that?"

"I told myself, I'm going to sit on the bed."

He sat next to her and stayed put. He smiled as if he'd run a marathon.

"I made an addendum to our will. We need three witnesses."

"Two."

"Three to be on the safe side. We have to make them co-conspirators."

"What do you know about co-conspirators?"

"Well, I put yesterday's date on everything. So we're cheating. Not a great way to start our redemption." She shrugged.

"Let me read it." Reggie moved to the desk and tried to pick up the papers. He wasn't successful.

She rushed forward and grabbed them, holding them behind her back.

"Remember what Raymond said?"

"Who's Raymond? Oh, yeah, the angel guy. Well, he said a lot of weird shit, which part?"

"We have to make amends before he comes back

for us. You realize he's trying to keep us out of hell . . . like Dante's hell . . . the hell . . . the place of fire and brimstone."

"Got it. He's some random guy. Maybe a ghost joking with us."

She glared at him. He sighed and sat on the bed and held out his hand.

"Let me read it."

"No, you have to trust me. I figured everything out while you were playing spook."

"I'm not going to like it."

"No you're not. But we're dead so what does it matter if we make positive changes."

"I don't like being dead."

"Reggie," she waved her arms around the room, "this is not hell. Let me fix this my way."

"I'm the boss."

She could have sworn that he put his lower lip out and pouted at her. It was hard to tell because he was almost completely invisible.

"I've made Eric the boss."

He groaned.

"He'll run the business into the ground. He'll be nice to people. He's a liberal snowflake. It won't work. I've worked my entire life to build this business."

"Yes, and we've been so mean and greedy that Raymond is going to send us to hell. Burn forever or let Eric fix things. Who of our children is most likely to make positive changes to get us into heaven."

He laid back on the bed and fell through. He sat up with his head in the middle of the bed. He sighed so loud it seemed to echo around the room.

He wasn't yelling or being himself. At that moment, she realized he never yelled at her and the kids. He yelled at everyone else as if they didn't matter to him. His kindness only extended to his immediate family.

She smiled at him. Maybe some part of him was okay with this.

"Hell. Fire. Brimstone. Agony for eternity."

"You know I don't believe in that stuff."

"Well, we also didn't believe in ghosts."

He laid back. This time he stayed on the bed. He looked up at the ceiling for a long time. Cynthia waited. No sense in annoying him until he made a decision.

He sat up. "All right."

"Good. Use your ectoplasm and go down stairs. Get Marta and whoever else is around. Don't tell them why they are coming up here. I'm going to pull a little sting."

"You're a little weird as a ghost. When did you get so bossy? And how do you know what a sting is?"

"I watch movies. I got bossy when I decided we aren't going to hell. Now go."

She wondered if lying and deceiving people for the greater good was a sin. In the movies she always hated it when the bad guys say they do things for the greater good. Now here she was doing something for the greater good.

Maybe she was cursing herself and Reggie.


## 5. CYNTHIA: FOR THE GREATER GOOD


She waited to turn back into her corporeal form until she heard Reggie and the others in the hallway talking. She placed the addendum in the desk drawer and turned the calendar to the previous day's date. Then she stood waiting for the door to open.

They were all laughing at something Reggie said. That by itself was odd. He hadn't joked around with the staff in years.

Marta wore the pink uniform with a white

apron. Her black hair was pulled neatly up in a bun. Her big brown eyes sparkled with amusement. She straightened as soon as she saw Cynthia.

Emily came in next wearing the same pink uniform. Her golden brown hair was also in a bun. She had a face an artist would love to paint, perfect symmetry with a nose that was slightly too big.

Cynthia realized the uniform was rather silly looking. They dressed exactly as she required. She wondered for a moment if she should also change a few things about herself as well as Reggie.

Pete, their full time handyman, came in last looking uncomfortable in his jean overalls. The smell of freshly sawed lumber followed him into the room. He'd always been shy and quiet. She imagined his neatly trimmed beard and his glasses were something he hid behind. He immediately removed his blue cap and gripped it tight in his calloused hands.

"Pete, please move the bench at the end of the bed closer to the desk so Marta and Emily can sit. And bring the chair by the window for you."

He carried the padded bench over and placed it so the women could sit.

"I'll stand. I wouldn't wanna get your nice chair dirty," Pete said.

She chose not to argue with him. He seemed more uncomfortable and nervous than usual.

"Marta, you have *brujas blancas* in your family, right?"

She glanced at Emily and Pete. Reggie smiled at her and nodded, encouraging her to answer. She clicked her lips.

"Yes, ma'am."

"You believe in ghosts, right?"

She nodded.

"Good. Reggie and I are ghosts."

Marta paled. Emily snorted. Pete lowered his head so she couldn't see his grin. Marta glanced at Reggie.

"I did see you earlier. In the kitchen," she said.

"Yes. I thought you saw me," Reggie grinned as if he were having fun. "We had an accident. Hit a tree. The kids should know soon. You'll hear about it."

"Reggie, give Pete and Emily a demonstration. I don't think they believe us."

He let his ectoplasm vanish. Emily jumped up.

"It is some kind of trick."

Reggie reappeared. "No, it's not." He turned and walked through the door and then came back into the room.

Pete crossed himself and took a step back. Then

he turned to Cynthia and squinted at her. She vanished and reappeared.

"*Dios mío*," Marta whispered. "You really are dead. What do you want with the living?"

"We are going to take you back one day and have you sign our will. We want to make changes, like giving you all a raise."

"A raise?" Reggie said.

Cynthia glared at him.

"Of course, a raise. That slipped my mind," Reggie said.

"Do you all agree?" Cynthia asked.

"This is a joke and magic trick." Emily shrugged. "I'll play along."

Marta and Pete nodded.

"Good. Stand up. Form a circle and take our hands."

Reggie stepped forward and grabbed Pete's and Emily's hands. Cynthia took Marta's hand.

"Your hand is very cold," Emily said.

Reggie shrugged. "Ghost. I guess we're cold."

"Now close your eyes."

When they all complied, Cynthia used her free hand to grab the bedspread. She shook and wrinkled it. "Take us back one day," she said in her best spooky voice.

Finally her thespian skills from college came in handy. Still shaking the bedspread, she waited a few seconds.

"Now. Okay, open your eyes."

Marta glanced at the rumpled bed, and her eyes grew wide. She jumped up and straightened the bedspread. Reggie grinned at Cynthia.

"Now, Reggie will sign the new will."

He dutifully made a show of signing. Then she did the same.

"Now, you are witnesses to the signing of the will. Each of you sign, and print your name under the signature."

Emily rolled her eyes and sat down first. She looked at the open calendar and placed her finger on the date. She glanced at Cynthia. She signed and printed her name. Pete went next. Then Marta, whose hands shook, sat down at the desk.

"Is this legal?" Marta asked.

"Yes, that's why I used my new powers to take you back in time. You are witnesses that we signed the will."

Marta glanced at Emily who nodded. Then she signed.

"Is that all?" Pete asked.

When she nodded, he turned toward the door.

"Wait," Cynthia shouted. "You can't leave yet. We must go back to the proper day. If you ran into yourselves, that could cause a terrible catastrophe to the time line."

Pete squinted at her and stepped back, moving closer to the others. Cynthia felt pleased with herself. She watched science fiction movies when Reggie wasn't around. Even Emily lost some of her skepticism.

As they formed a circle, they held hands again. When everyone's eyes were closed, Cynthia released Reggie's hand and flipped the calendar back to the proper date.

"Take us back to our proper time." Cynthia counted to five in her mind. "We're back. You can open your eyes."

She was tempted to say something dramatic, maybe a prophecy or something. But she dismissed the idea. Best to keep things simple and get this over with before they ran out of ectoplasm.

Reggie cleared his throat. "Now, you must vow that you will not tell our children, the lawyers, and anyone else that we went back in time."

"Of course not," Pete said. "Everyone would think we were crazy, and the will wouldn't be valid."

Once they'd left, she folded the pages and placed them in a manila envelope. She handed it to Reggie.

"Address it to Eric. Sign your name and put yesterday's date beside your name."

"What are you up to? No one will believe this."

"Of course, they will. Marta's a believer. Emily saw the calendar. My ploy with Pete freaked him out a little. Plus, Pete understands that they can't tell anyone they traveled back in time to sign the will. He's right, people would think they're crazy. They'll just say they signed yesterday."

"We'll see," he said as he sat at the desk and addressed the envelope to their youngest son. "Can I read it now?"

"No. I think our first day as ghosts should be pleasant. Let's turn into ghosts and take a walk around the grounds. We can hold hands like we used to do."

He immediately vanished, but she could see his shimmering form.

"I say we walk through doors and walls," he said. "It'll be fun. This ghost thing isn't as bad as I thought it would be."

"What's gotten into you?" Cynthia asked as she let go of her ectoplasm.

Reggie took her hand and led her to the door, which they floated through.

"I don't know what's gotten into me. I'm dead, so why not see if your plan works. Owen and Hannah are going to be pissed. Maybe they'll sue Eric."

"They won't," Cynthia said. "I'll threaten to haunt them forever."

Reggie chuckled. They walked hand in hand through doors and into the kitchen, where Marta and Emily sat at the counter talking about them.

Marta pointed to them. "They're here."

"Don't worry," Reggie said. "Enjoy your break. We're just taking a walk. Hell, take the day off. There's no one to cook for. Do something fun."

"No, no, we cannot. Hannah and Owen are on their way over. They phoned. They know you are dead. Poor dears are very upset," Emily said.

"We'll tell them all about it later. That's nice of you to stay," Cynthia said. "Thank you."

Once they got outside, Reggie looked at her and shook his head. "You thanked the cook for doing her job."

"I'm developing good will. You should try it."

"I suggested they take the day off. That's good will."

"You are absolutely right." Cynthia smiled.

They walked by the shop where Pete had opera playing in the background. Reggie appeared for a moment and waved at Pete, who stared and finally nodded. They strolled toward the pond, which Cynthia thought could easily be considered a small lake.

It was stocked with fish, had a small dock and a shed with fishing gear. No one had used it since the kids left home. She glanced back at the house and the extensive grounds. She'd always thought the house should be filled with people who would enjoy the grounds.

People playing tennis, swimming in the pool, those were the sorts of things she'd like to see. There were so many fun things to do that they never did.

"Let's be solid," Reggie said as his corporeal body materialized.

She did the same. A breeze with the fragrance of jasmine lifted her hair. She could feel the breeze and smell the flowers. Somehow that made her happy. When Hannah was small, she used to pick the little jasmine flowers and put them in her hair.

"Mama, look at the pretty flowers," Hannah would call out.

Cynthia realized they would have to break the news of their ghost state to the children. She wasn't entirely sure how they should do that. She hoped by the time they walked to the river and back, she'd have a plan.

At least the children were young enough that having a heart attack at seeing their dead parents shouldn't be a problem.

At some point, Reggie might revert back to his old self. She'd need a plan for that, just in case. The best case would be that he'd continue enjoying being a ghost.

She did remember that he used to like to play pranks on people. Maybe she could encourage that. He could be like Puck, a mischievous ghost.

# 6. ERIC: THE ADDENDUM

Eric stood in the middle of his parents' bedroom. His parents had somehow moved through the bed and walked through walls. The huge red and gold fan painted with dragons had been knocked lopsided on the wall.

He'd arrived at his parents' house to find Owen and Hannah ecstatic with joy. Yes, they were dead, but they were ghosts. Eric immediately tried to reason with them. That was before his parents appeared.

What followed was craziness. Reluctantly he was left with the conclusion that his parents were ghosts.

Could he admit that to anyone? Could he admit it to himself? Was he going crazy?

These were serious questions.

Somehow his brain couldn't fully process anything. His father was definitely not himself. He acted ridiculously cheerful. He insisted that Marta, Emily, and Pete call him Reggie.

Eric found himself watching his parents, analyzing every move they made. Not believing in anything supernatural and then suddenly believing in ghosts caused his brain to play tricks on him. One second he embraced the idea, the next his mind revolted.

So that's how he wound up himself sitting next to Emily and listening to his mother, who held a manila envelope. He clasped the rough brocade fabric of his chair and wondered if he were the only person losing his mind.

The staff, Hannah, and Owen believed their story. Of course, he could smell alcohol on Owen's breath, so he wasn't reliable.

His mother handed him the envelope. He ran his hand over the smooth surface of the paper. Somehow the tactile experiences helped ground him. If he felt the thing, it must be real.

"That's an addendum to our will," Cynthia said.

He stared at his father's handwriting. Seeing his name and address spelled out also helped him focus. He couldn't understand how one second his parents had corporeal bodies and the next they didn't.

His mother kept talking about ectoplasm as if he should know what she was talking about.

What he knew was that to write an addendum, they had to be able to pick up a pen and write. In his confused mind, ghosts were supposed to be non-corporeal. Until five minutes ago, he would have sworn that ghosts didn't exist.

"When did you write this?" Eric asked.

"Why does that matter?" Hannah said. "Just do your lawyer stuff."

"When?" Eric watched his father.

"Yesterday, dear," Cynthia said. "It's all legal. Marta, Emily, and Pete signed as witnesses."

"Why did you write this yesterday?"

"Because I had a feeling. You know, the sixth sense. It happens to people."

Eric glanced at his father, who shrugged. His father knew they couldn't have an addendum made after their death. No one in their right minds would believe he and his siblings didn't forge this. Yet, he was supposed to believe his parents somehow managed to prepare for their deaths one day ahead of time.

He wondered what they were up to. If all this was true, they'd set up their kids for huge legal battles.

"Marta, Pete, Emily, you signed these papers yesterday?"

Marta nodded.

"Yes," Emily said and nudged Pete, who agreed.

"You didn't think this was strange?" Eric watched Pete, who was the least likely to be part of a scam.

"Yes, we did." Pete shrugged. "But we did as they asked."

"What part did you think was strange?" Eric wasn't going to give up. The last thing he wanted was to be part of some ruse his father planned.

Pete scratched his head. "Well, it was Mrs. Keller, I mean Cynthia. She was all business-like, planning things and doing all the talking."

"Why are you asking all these questions?" Hannah asked. "Just open the thing and read it."

Eric ignored her. "One more question. Mom, why did you write this?"

Cynthia Keller took a deep breath and exhaled. She smiled at her son and glanced at Reggie.

"Well, for about three weeks, I was thinking about telling your father I wanted to leave. Not get a divorce, but move to our vacation home."

"What?" Reggie jumped up.

"Oh, for heaven's sake, sit down," Cynthia said. "We'll talk about it later."

To Eric's surprise, his father sat. Hannah stared at her mother.

Owen whispered, "I need a drink."

His brother's breath reeked of booze.

"Well," Cynthia said, "that got me thinking about Aunt Eugenia leaving Uncle Nathan. Her plane crashed on her way home."

Okay. His mother did this. She spoke about unconnected events as if they held some connected meaning. Eric was losing his patience.

"So, I thought, what if something happened to one of us or both? You know I always say to follow your gut feelings. We needed a will that straightened out the business. So, we can made things better for the workers and their families."

Her explanation didn't make sense, but at this point he should probably just open the envelope and read it. Which he did.

If yesterday, someone had told him his father would turn into a benevolent man, he would have laughed. This addendum laid out a plan to turn all their businesses into businesses focused on the employees. He glanced at the dates and the signatures. It was simple. Would it hold up in court?

"Dad, you signed this and agree with the contents."

"I signed it, but I didn't read it."

Eric closed his eyes. Beside him Owen cleared his throat.

"Pops, you told me never to sign anything without reading it first."

"Yes, Owen, the best advice I ever gave you."

"Then why didn't you read it?" Hannah leaned forward looking very much like she doubted that was possible.

"I was in a hurry. She told me not to read it because I wouldn't agree. I said no. She insisted. I had a meeting, so I signed it. I figured I'd tear it up later. Then I watched those three sign it."

"You still haven't read it? It's legal and binding."

Eric watched his father smile at his mother. "Still haven't read it."

"This will give me control over making changes. It specifies that Zoe will come in and help make changes.

"Oh, Cynthia, Zoe, really? She's—"

"Don't say it, dear. Who better to help Eric, Owen, and Hannah make positive changes." His mother managed to look both happy and clueless.

"But Zoe?" Reggie asked.

"Yes, Zoe."

Now, Eric definitely believed his father didn't read it. If he knew Zoe was involved, he'd never have signed it. If there were two people in the world who never saw eye to eye, Reggie and Zoe were those two people.

"Dad, why aren't you upset about this?"

"I'm dead. I figure the worst has happened.

"Not the worst, dear," Cynthia said. "There's alway hell."

"Well, yes. There is that."

At the mention of hell, Hannah and Owen both chimed in talking at once. When his parents started trying to explain, the room seemed to explode in nonstop unanswerable questions.

Eric walked into the hallway and sat on the floor outside his parents' room. The floor was the same white and gold marble as downstairs. It was smooth and cold to the touch as he sat.

He slowly read and reread the addendum. This gave him control of the entire enterprise and brought Zoe in to help. His mother planned to raise employees' salaries, get better healthcare, and build a free daycare for working families. He blinked several times and reread the document.

He realized they could change everything that he disliked about his father's businesses. She even mentioned a college trust fund. Helping kids get through college was something he could back. Being on the board, he knew how much money the corporation had. Enough to do all this and more.

He'd come here to step away from the businesses. Somehow that didn't matter anymore. He reread the document.

Some part of him was excited about this. Another part of his brain told him he was getting sucked into the business. This was exactly what his father wanted. But . . . yes, there were some buts. He could help make things better and later turn everything over to Owen and Hannah. No, they couldn't keep something this big going. But he could teach them.

That's when he knew he'd decided to stay. It wasn't a small job. It would take years. Yet, he was excited. This was the craziest thing he'd ever heard of anyone doing. He'd do it.

The roasted chicken smell coming from the kitchen reminded him he was hungry. They could eat and talk things over, find out exactly what his parents wanted to do.

Pete stepped into the hall and looked down at him.

"Mind if I join you?"

"No. Take a seat."

Pete with a sly grin and his overalls smelling like sawdust sat cross-legged beside him.

"You know what's in this?" Eric asked.

Pete shook his head. "I got an idea. I know a couple things you should know. I'm just a simple man, but I listen more than I talk."

Eric chuckled. "Pete, you're anything but a simple man. My father does a background check on everyone he hires. I know you owned A Slice of Life. I also know you were very wealthy. I know you walked away from it all and changed your name."

As Eric spoke, Pete's smile grew wider and wider. He nodded.

"Yeah, all that's true."

"Why?"

"Well, my goal when I started was to make people's lives better. If you live long enough you see great businesses that want to do good. They go on for years like that. Then they forget their better angles or things just change. They get labeled as evil." Pete chuckled. "Maybe not evil, but not good."

"I've never heard you talk so much," Eric said.

"I talk when I have somethin' to say."

"I think advice is coming my way. Go on."

"I've been watching your mother grow unhappy. I think she looked around and saw things were not so good with the business. She really wanted to leave. That's what happened to me. I took my corporation public, and although I had a controlling interest, everything turned into the bottom line. All that mattered was money. My wife was okay with that. I wasn't. I gave her almost everything and left."

Eric leaned his head against the wall. He should probably listen to Pete. The idea of making things right appealed to him. He'd love to help the people of this town and make the various businesses something to be proud of.

"So are you saying I should take the businesses, make them better, and don't go public?"

Pete nodded. Back to his old self. A man of few words.

"So, did you really sign these papers yesterday?"

Pete nodded.

"That's a little hard to believe."

"It is. Another thing that's hard to believe is that a man, maybe an angel, came to your parents after the accident and said he'd give them eight years to redeem themselves by fixing the bad things they've done."

Eric sat up straighter. Somehow this day just got a little stranger.

"You believe in angels?"

Pete scratched his head. "I never did before, but I also didn't believe in ghosts. So maybe. If they're right, you got yourself two ghosts for the next few years."

That put a whole new spin on things. An angel offering his parents redemption made sense. Maybe that's why his father had changed so much.

"You believe in hell?" Eric asked.

"Not a literal place. People manage to do enough bad to make the here and now into a sort of hell."

"I came here to tell my father I was resigning. I want to help people."

Pete tapped on the papers in Eric's hand. "Looks like you got an offer to do some good."

"You're right. If I need advice, can I come to you?"

"I'll give you advice if I can. Don't know much about all the businesses your father started. Right now you need to know that Owen's in a bad place. His wife left him, took the kids. He's drinking too much. Maybe drugs. I'm guessing about that. Hannah has good ideas and dreams. Your father's beaten them both down. Help them find their dreams again."

"Thanks."

"I think you should all go downstairs and eat something. Let Marta and Emily go home to their families." Pete stood up. "Those two ghosts are going to give you a run for your money. Good luck."

Eric went to sleep wondering if he'd wake up in the morning and realize he'd been dreaming.


## 7. CYNTHIA: AN EXPLANATION

The moon shone bright, but only a little reached into the covered patio, creating a semi-darkness. The small solar lights in the flower bed did little more than create atmosphere. Cynthia sat in the rattan chair across from Reggie. The tan pillows on the rattan furniture looked gray.

She could see fire without turning on the lights, which she guessed was a perk of ghosthood.

She watched Reggie with interest. They were conserving ectoplasm so no one could see them, but they could see each other. The only way she could describe seeing him was with the word "weird."

He looked very much like himself but not himself. They were a sort grayish image of their former selves. She wondered if they went to the cemetery in Bluefield if they'd run into other ghosts. Would they be a strange form somewhere between a corporeal body and a hazy human shape?

All her thinking about ghosts and ectoplasm was a way to avoid answering Reggie's question. He'd asked her if she was really planning on leaving him. It was out of the bag, so she couldn't sidestep the issue.

Finally, she took a deep breath and exhaled. Only weird thing was she didn't feel her lungs or the air when she tried to inhale or exhale. Apparently in her state, breathing wasn't a thing.

"Are you going to answer me?" Reggie had a habit of smirking, which he was doing as he watched her.

"Yes. I was planning on leaving. I wasn't happy. I thought I'd go to the vacation home. It's nice there."

"You don't love me?" Reggie looked down at his grayish hands and then looked up at her.

"I've always loved you. That'll never change."

"Then why?"

She reached out to take his hand, but he pulled away.

"Remember when we were young, you wanted a people-friendly business? You said. 'Let's make the world better.' So we lived in a tiny apartment, waited to have kids, and both worked, saving our money."

He grinned. "Sure. When we saved enough money, we bought that old building and fixed it up. We opened the first coffee shop in Bluefield."

"I remember the poets, the authors, and the young musicians. Remember that skinny kid who told jokes that had people laughing. What was her name."

"How could you forget her name. Winifred. She had that silly joke about her mother wanting a boy and a girl. Since she could only have one child, she named her Wini for the girl half and Fred for the boy half. Sounds stupid when I say it."

"Yeah, somehow she made it sound funny. People came from all over because the coffee house was fun. They came and forgot about their worries. We helped a few people, artists, poets, and writers. Some launched their careers in our little coffee shop."

He sat back on the lounge chair and folded his arms behind his head. Staring off into the distance, he grinned. Somehow his gray body looked younger, happier.

"Yeah, before we knew it, we had six coffee shops around Washington. Course, we had to open bookstores."

He glanced at her.

"I guess those were the good old days," he said. Of course then along came those other coffee places. They got big. We struggled. Then we scrambled and started a new business. We were always doing something."

"Yes, Reggie. We were happy then. When you fuss at Eric, you forget he's just like you. You were always trying to figure out ways to help people."

He sat up and leaned over and took her hand. "You're right, I forgot all that. How did I change?"

"Slowly, until both of us were only about the

money. Money, money, money," she said. "You know just before the accident, you told Dave to tell some woman to hire a babysitter. I wanted to shake you and remind you that she didn't make enough money to hire a sitter. We pay wages no one can live on."

He shook his head. "You're right. I never intended for things to change. Money became like a game. The people with the most money win."

He frowned. The frown deepened as he stared at his hands. "I made a good life for us."

"It wasn't a good life for our employees. Or for me. Before, I felt like we were doing something good. When we built this house, I started realizing we had lost our joy. Money can buy things, but we had more than enough."

"So you were going to leave because we were too rich? Because the house was too fancy?"

"No, I was going to leave because we lost our way. Remember the dreams about making our little part of the world better for people? We weren't thinking of mansions or how much money we had. We loved the coffee house. We laughed, met new people, artists, poets, and musicians spent their weekend entertaining our customers."

Cynthia chuckled. "Remember that singer, the one who got popular, and later died in a car crash? I forgot his name. When Hannah got sick, he sent us money for the hospital bill. That's when we decided we needed insurance for our employees."

"You remember his name. You're trying to jog my memory. Eric was his name. We named Eric after him."

"You're right. I'm trying to get you to remember who we used to be."

Reggie stared off into the night for a long time. The minutes ticked by and Cynthia thought about going back inside. He was too wrapped up in his old ways. She could remind him that Raymond gave them a few years to make things right.

She knew appealing to the very human desire not to go to Hell would be cheating. If they were going to change, he needed to see a way forward. So she let him stare into the night.

When he finally spoke, she started and sat up straighter.

"I lost my way," Reggie said. "I love you. You're right. I just don't know how to go back and find my old self."

She reached over and took his hand. "One step at a time. That's what you used to say. We do it one step at a time."

"Do you still want to leave?"

"I don't think that's the right question," she said. "We're dead. That changes everything. We have a chance to find our old selves, do some good, and see our children happy and following their dreams."

"I guess the right question is, do you want to stay here and help me turn things around?"

Cynthia chuckled. "I do. I have wanted that for years, but I couldn't find the man I used to know and love. You know money's not a thing anymore. Do you hate my plan?"

"No . . . except for Zoe. She called me a capitalist bully."

When he said that, he laughed. At first it was a chuckle. Then it grew into a full belly laugh. Then Cynthia caught the laughing bug. A few minutes later they calmed down.

He shook his head. "She was right. I was bullying her. Actually, I was trying to get her to quit. I hate firing people. But I lost my temper and fired her. Called her a liberal snowflake commie. Not very original. I was terrible. She might not want to help Eric."

"You could always apologize. We'll have to let her know we are ghosts."

"Eat crow?" He shook his head. "I'm not good at

that. But I'm willing to try. Can't wait to see her face when she sees me."

That reminded Cynthia. Funeral. They had to have a funeral. She could plan it and then the kids wouldn't have to go through all that trouble.

"Reggie, have we made funeral arrangements?"

"No. I guess we should have thought about that. The kids will take care of it."

"No. I'm going to plan it, and you are going to help me. I think we should plan it like a big party."

"Sure thing."

Cynthia squinted at him. "Why are you being so co-operative?"

Reggie stood up and held out his hand.

"Let's go for a walk. Like I told the kids, I'm dead. None of the living stuff matters. Maybe I'm tired of being a capitalist bully."

She took his hand, and he led her out onto the grass. After a few steps, he turned toward the house and pointed.

"Look at that monstrosity. Two of us were rattling around in that place. It should be full of people."

"I think Hannah wants to turn it into an inn," Cynthia said.

Reggie leaned over and kissed her. "That sounds

like a wonderful idea. She should do that. You wanna go skinny dipping?"

"That sounds like a lovely idea."

They played Marco Polo until the sun came up. Whoever caught the other got a kiss. It turned out that kissing was still fun. She might not be able to feel herself breathing. But her libido worked just fine, so did Reggie's.

She couldn't remember the last time they'd had so much fun.

**Short story Collections:**

*Christmas Magic: 5 Original Holiday Shorts Stories*

*Have Portal. Will Travel: 5 Original Short Stories set in the League of the Daring World.*

*Short Stories*

Buy directly from Cora at corafoerstner.com or woodsorrelstudios.com. Her books are available in major online retailers; use this link to find her books at your preferred retail store: https://books2read.com/corafoerstner/

# ABOUT THE AUTHOR

Cora Foerstner wanted to be a spy when she was a teenager. Danger, adventure, and exotic places sounded amazing. Since that life didn't pan out, she figured the next best thing would be to tell stories about adventure, danger, mysteries, awesome places, and people she wished were real.

When Cora isn't writing science fiction and fantasy stories, she plays video games, drinks lots of coffee and green tea, and researches things like dragons, climate change, the end of the world, and other unsavory subjects. She is a super fangirl of the Expanse Series (Books & TV). She never misses a superhero movie.

Find out more about her other books, go to corafoerstner.com or woodsorrelstudios.com. Her books are also available on all major online retailers. Find her books on your favorite book store: https://books2read.com/CoraFoerstner